Dancing in Circles

A Step in Time Book two

Second edition

Stacey Broadbent

Dancing in Circles (2nd Edition)
Published by Stacey Broadbent
Copyright © 2021 Stacey Broadbent

First published 2014
Re-released 2018

Proofreading by Spell Bound
Cover image from Deposit Photos
Cover Design by Stacey Broadbent

ISBN: 978-0-473-58317-0 (paperback)
         978-0-473-58318-7 (MOBI)

For Petrina and Dena,
Thank you for all your encouragement and inspiration.

Dance as though no one is watching

Contents

Chapter 1

"Will you stop anticipating?" Dane threw his hands in the air.

"I'm not anticipating, I'm following. Maybe if you led me correctly, I would do whatever it is you are trying to get me to do!" Maddi was sick of listening to him complain about her dancing. She was every bit as good as he was, if not better.

They had competed together in the National Salsa Competitions the previous year and come out on top in their category. This year they planned on doing the same. The pressure was on though, as there was some fierce competition. Sacha and Jessie—who came a close second place—had made it known they were working on something big and had been all year. They were good. More than good, they could actually win; there had only been a few points between them. But Dane was determined to put them in their place this year. It was sweet at the top, and he intended on staying there.

"I am leading. You're not following!" He hit the bench, making Maddi jump.

"You know what? You need to cool down. I'm not dancing with you like this." She turned to walk away, but he grasped her arm, pulling her towards him.

"I'm sorry, okay? I just want to win so bad. I couldn't stand to see that smug bitch, Sacha, beat us." Maddi smiled and reached her arms up to caress his neck. He and Sacha had a history together. They had been dance partners (and more) when they first started out. They were practically inseparable from the moment they met at their first salsa class… until Sacha met Jessie that is. He had been a friend of Danes who took to dance like a fish to water. To his credit, Jessie had fought off her advances at first, she was just so damn persistent. Once she had someone in her sights, there was no way to resist her. Dane didn't blame Jessie, not anymore. He knew the powerful intoxication she possessed with her pouty lips and seductive eyes.

What he didn't expect was for her to take his routine and use it against him in the competitions. He had actually forgiven them both for their betrayal until that moment. Watching them do the routine he had poured so much of himself into, had made his blood boil. If it hadn't been for Maddi standing by his side, holding his hand and keeping him focused, he probably would've caused a scene. Instead, he'd channelled all of that negative energy and they'd pulled off the best performance of their lives. Now, just the thought of Sacha beating him was enough to get him all hot and bothered.

"Baby, we beat them last year, we can do it again," she soothed, stroking the wisps of hair at the base of his neck. "You know we'll kick arse. I mean, come on, you have me as your partner." She grinned up at him as she felt him relax into her.

"You're awesome, you know that?" His lips skimmed hers. "And gorgeous…" She felt the warmth of his breath on her neck as he nuzzled her, his thoughts clearly on other things.

"None of that. We have work to do. This routine won't come together on its own." She eased herself out of his grip.

"Slave driver."

"You know you like it. Now, where were we?"

They continued to practice through the night, but Maddi could see Dane's mind wasn't really on it. He was more than a little obsessed with the desire to win. No, not just to win, but to hurt Sacha. That was what it really boiled down to, and Maddi knew it. At first, she didn't mind his dedication, but it was starting to take its toll. There was only so much you could hear about an ex before it got on your nerves. Not to mention, Dane wouldn't let Maddi help with choreography. She had so many great ideas for the new routine, but Dane was so stubborn that he dismissed them before she even got a chance to share them. Sure, he was the more experienced salsa dancer, but that's not always what makes you the strongest dancer.

Maddi believed in learning other styles and incorporating them into your dance; blending techniques. When she was a child, she had taken jazz, rock 'n' roll, and even a little Irish—you know the kind where your body is still, while your feet are moving at 50mph? She had always liked the look of salsa, and after a messy break up, decided to give it a go. It only took one lesson before she was hooked. She went to as many classes as she could manage; even some workshops with international teachers to learn some new styles that were becoming popular. It wasn't long before she had been asked to join a ladies' troupe where they choreographed 'shine' routines—where you dance solo, but in a team—so no partners needed. She had been dancing every day of the week; training by day and social dancing by night. Her teacher had taken her under her wing and introduced her to everyone worth knowing in the dance scene. This was how she'd met Dane, and after a few dances together, they'd realised how well they gelled. From then on, they had been partners.

Their relationship didn't blossom until that night at the comps. Maddi had seen the anger flash in his eyes as he watched Sacha and Jessie execute the routine he'd choreographed. She knew that he would be too distracted to dance, so she did the only thing she could think of. She grabbed his hand, pulled him aside, and kissed him. It certainly took his mind off his ex, for a while at least. They had been together ever since. Not exactly your fairy tale love story, and definitely not the way Maddi had intended for things to happen. You work with what you've got though, right?

Secretly, she had been working on a solo routine to pull out at the comps this year. She felt confident she had a shot at placing, if not winning. Maddi loved dancing more than anything, and all she wanted was to express herself through dance. She could see that that was never going to happen with Dane squashing her ideas, and that was when she made the decision to work on her own routine as well. Maybe Dane would take her seriously once he saw what she could really do.

"I don't know about this."

"Oh, come on, how bad can it be? It's not like we don't know anyone here. We'll just try it for one night, and if you're not happy then we can go back to Latin Flava, okay?" Maddi practically dragged Dane up the stairs to the dance studio. After much discussion, she had finally convinced him to see if perhaps they could pick up some new moves for their routine. She had seen the performance troupe doing their thing at one of the social nights and had been dying to try them out ever since. "They have a unique style. I think we could really use some of it to spice things up a bit." Dane rolled his eyes at her.

"You and your 'style'. What's so wrong with the way I dance?"

"Don't be like that. You know that's not what I'm meaning. I just think we will have an advantage if we broaden our skills." She waited a beat before adding, "If you want to beat Sacha, this is the best way to do it and you know it. She's far too arrogant to take lessons from anyone else." With that, she pushed through the doors and headed towards the teacher to introduce herself. She could hear the whispers as she walked by.

"Is that who I think it is?"

"I heard they're competing again this year."

"What do you think they're doing here?"

"I guess we'll find out soon enough. Oh, I'd love it if they were going to teach!"

Maddi smiled; they were well recognised in the salsa scene after winning last year, and the attention had yet to diminish. She got such a kick out of it. I mean, who wouldn't? Knowing that there were so many girls out there who would give anything to move like her—or have the confidence to do so—and to have a dance partner who could match you. It's not easy to find someone who matches your skill level, style, *and* is the right height.

Maddi had just kind of fell into a partnership with Dane after a drunken night with a bunch of dancers that her teacher had introduced her to. Even after all the drinks, they had still been able to dance together, and well. The rest, as they say, is history.

"All right, everyone! Gather round! We are lucky enough to have some fabulous dancers joining us this evening. For those of you who don't know them, Dane and Maddi won the intermediate section at the Nationals last year." Lisa beamed at them. "Perhaps we could persuade them to do a freestyle for us after class?" There was a lot of clapping and cheering. Amusement danced in Dane's eyes. If there was anything that could bring him out of his mood, a boost to his ego would be it.

"Sure, no worries, we can bust out some moves for ya." He winked at Lisa as he pulled her in for a dip, holding her just long enough for her to get flustered. Always the ladies' man was Dane. It was one of the reasons he had started dancing in the first place—to get the girls. He loved the attention that came with being able to move in time to the beat—you'd be surprised how many guys have no idea of rhythm, and girls were only too happy to share that with him. They were enamoured with his moves and couldn't get enough of him. Of course, he was with Maddi now, but as far as he was concerned there was nothing wrong with a bit of flirting. Maddi got annoyed every now and again, but she knew it was all in fun, she was his after all. Sure, sometimes he would let his hand linger a little too long or pull them in for a cuddle and hold just that little bit tighter, but she was the only one who got to go home with him. The way he saw it, she should feel privileged that he was willing to be with her. She had been a nothing until he came along and made her into the dancer she is today. Other girls would kill to be in her shoes.

Class turned out to be better than they had expected. Dane seemed to be enjoying himself, and Maddi had done as she had set out to do—learn new material. With a bit of luck, she wouldn't have to work so hard to get Dane to come along to a class next time. As much as he'd like to think he was God's gift to dance, he didn't know all the moves. It was impossible when dance is forever evolving.

As promised, they did an impromptu freestyle performance, which was well received. Several girls came up to Maddi afterwards to ask for some tips on styling. She was more than happy to help. One of the things she loved most about them being titleholders, was that she could be an inspiration to others. She never would have made it this far, had she not been taken under the wing of her teacher, Rachel, and now it was her chance to 'pay it forward' and help other girls find their potential. She was good at it too, never making people feel silly for asking, and always finding time to help.

Lisa was watching her do this while she went about closing up for the night.

"You're good with them, you know. Have you ever thought about teaching?"

"Me? It hadn't really crossed my mind. I'm not qualified or anything."

"You don't need to be. They love you. I've seen the way you are with them. These girls would follow you anywhere." She smiled warmly.

"Oh… My… God! You have to!" squealed the brunette standing next to Maddi. "I would love to learn from you! You're sooooo good, and you make it look really sexy. I wish I could get my hips to move like yours," she gushed. Maddi's cheeks flushed as she smiled warmly.

"Well, I can hardly let down my fans now, can I?"

Lisa winked at the brunette. "That's great. When can you start? Maybe you could do a styling class for the ladies, and then you and Dane could teach some partner moves? I know a few of the guys would be keen to learn from him. The studio has had a recent influx of students, and I don't have enough teachers, you'd be doing me a huge favour."

"Sure, sounds like fun. I'll talk to Dane tonight, and we can sort out a time. I'd be keen to start up whenever you'll have me."

The brunette jumped up and down excitedly, "Yay! I can't wait to tell Piper, she's gonna go mental!"

Chapter 2

Maddi stared at her reflection as she tried to mentally psych herself up for her first ever teaching gig. With her ice-blue eyes and bouncing blonde curls, she was a knockout. While most girls would give anything to have her stunning beauty, she felt it was more of a burden. Sure, she could get into clubs at an earlier age and often had guys falling at her feet to go out with her, but it wasn't all it was cracked up to be. She'd had her fair share of guys trying to get in her pants and then some. It had led to the occasional obsessive guy who couldn't take no for an answer. Not to mention the jealousy of other girls. She saw the way they looked at her when she was anywhere near their boyfriends—as if she was trying to lure them away. It made it hard for her to make friends.

Rory was the only one who wasn't paranoid. They had been best friends since preschool, ever since Rory had come to her rescue after one of the other girls had shoved Maddi. She was headstrong and not afraid of anything. Maddi looked up to her, wishing she could be more like that herself. She cared too much what people thought of her, leaving her feeling as if she was never quite good enough.

Pulling on a crimson, merino sweater, she took one last look at herself and headed out the door. It was her ladies styling class tonight, and she wanted to be there early to go over a few things. To say she was nervous was an understatement. She hoped she had enough material to last them the full hour. Dane was going to be there, teaching men's footwork at the other end of the studio. They were to join up in the last hour to teach some partner work—a move of his choice, of course.

When she opened the doors to the studio, she was pleasantly surprised by how many people had shown up already for their classes. The place was packed! She couldn't quite believe that they were all there to see *her*. If only she wasn't so nervous.

Walking over to one of the spare seats, she attempted to calm herself. *Come on, Maddi, you can do this! They all believe in you, so now you have to believe in yourself. You got this!*

She put her dance heels on, grabbed her iPod and headed for the front of the room. She could feel their eyes watching her every move. *Don't trip, don't trip, don't trip.*

Clearing her throat, she began, "Alright, everyone. Ah, if you're here for ladies styling then gather round and we'll get started." She smiled as they moved into position. "Okay, so we'll start with a warmup, just like in class, only we'll be doing ladies steps this time—we are ladies after all." There was a smatter of laughter, and the tension fell from her shoulders. She could do this.

"We'll then move on to some styling techniques that you can use in both your solo dancing and your partner dancing. I'll show you several different options, and hopefully there will be something for everyone."

The music began, and the last of her inhibitions dissipated. She relaxed into the music, her body on autopilot. It was what she loved most about dancing—losing herself to the music. Watching her students in the mirror, she could see there were some others who felt the same way.

"Good. Feel the music, let it wash over you. You need to let go and just let it happen." She found that the more they got into it, the more they gave her. She was pushing them, and they were responding to every instruction, every movement. By the end of the session, they were all glowing.

"Well done, everyone. I hope you enjoyed it as much as I did. Keep practicing those body isolations; we'll be doing more work on that next week. If you are staying for the next class with Dane and I, then have a quick drink, and we'll get back into it."

What a rush! Maddi had never felt more alive than she did at that moment. The pure joy of dancing and sharing that with others; there was nothing quite like it. She couldn't believe she was actually being paid to do this. What more could she possibly want from life?

After a brief drink break and a few words to some of the girls, she was ready to get into the next class. Looking around, she was happy to see some new faces among the 'regulars' who graced the social floors.

"Gather round, everyone! We've got a big class tonight so split into a few rows for the warmup. Make sure you can see us. We'll rotate the rows throughout the song." Dane put on some music and called out the steps. Once he got to the more difficult moves it was easy to spot who the newcomers were. Maddi gave him a *take it easy* look, which he ignored. Any chance to show off. If he kept this up, they'd lose them.

"Alright, for those of you who haven't done a lot of shine work, just continue doing basics if you don't know the steps. Dane can get a little carried away sometimes." Maddi smiled sweetly at him. *That should bring him down a peg or two.* "Now if everyone can grab their partners and make a circle, that would be great. If you don't have a partner, you can slot in between a couple, and we will rotate around so that everyone gets a chance to try the moves." She dragged Dane into the centre of the circle. "This is the move we will be doing tonight, just watch this time, and then we'll break it down." She looked up at Dane, ready for him to take the lead. The look in his eyes told her he was not happy with her. *Oh great, what's he going to do now?* He grabbed her, a little tighter than was necessary.

Smiling, he bent down to whisper, "Don't *ever* try to embarrass me like that again." His smile never wavering, he straightened up and began the move. He changed it from what they had rehearsed, obviously trying to trip her up, but she was prepared and followed him faultlessly, which pissed him off even more. He could be so petty sometimes. Maddi was not about to let him intimidate her; she was a professional and she would teach this class with or without his help. She took the lead and began to break down the move. After each part, she would work her way around the room to make sure everyone was grasping the steps before moving onto the next stage. There were some great dancers; a few even adapted the moves to suit their own style, which really impressed her. One guy in particular stood out from the rest. He'd seemed so reserved at the beginning of class; Maddi had hardly noticed him, but once he started moving, he was beautiful to watch. She could tell he was nervous when it was her turn to dance with him, so she attempted to keep it light.

"Don't think of me as the teacher, I'm just a girl wanting to dance, like all the others." She could see a hint of a smile as he lifted his eyes to meet hers.

"Yeah sure, just a girl who could dance circles around anyone in this room. No, that's not intimidating at all." He grinned back at her, his face lighting up.

God, he's gorgeous! That cheeky grin and those beautiful brown eyes. I could just melt into them. She had to force herself to turn her eyes away and stop staring before she made him uncomfortable. Laughing, she reached for his hand.

"No need to be intimidated, I'm nothing special. Like I said, 'I'm just a girl', now dance with me."

"Yes, Ma'am."

"Ma'am?" She stood back, her hands on her hips. "How old do you think I am?" she joked, "Call me Maddi."

"Alright then, Maddi, I'm Ricki." He pulled her in to begin the move. She had never had to concentrate so hard to follow in her life. The smell of his cologne, the feel of his hands; it was all rather distracting. And he thought *she* was intimidating. She should be calling out for people to switch partners, but she was enjoying herself too much with Ricki. He had such a nice style and was eager to learn. It was refreshing to dance with someone who was in no way arrogant. Dane had been like that once. It's amazing how much a little attention can change someone.

Speak of the devil. When his eyes landed on her and Ricki, his chest puffed out. Not wanting her to be enjoying the arms of another man so much, he quickly put an end to it.

"Right, everyone, I think that's enough for tonight. You all picked that up well. We might have to come up with something trickier for next week to really challenge you. Don't forget there is a social night in town tomorrow at Feeney's Bar from 9pm. I hope to see you all out there." He was laying it on thick, like he always did, trying to charm people. It generally worked too; Maddi had seen it all too often.

"So, I guess that's it then." Ricki pulled away and automatically shifted back into shy awkwardness.

"Yeah, I guess so. Thanks for the dance, you're better than you think, you know?" She touched his arm. "Will you come tomorrow night? Feeney's is pretty cool. They play great music, and the floor is huge." She looked at him hopefully. "We could go over the move some more if you like. Or just fool around… on the dancefloor I mean." Her face was on fire as she tried to laugh it off. *Oh…My…God, could I be more embarrassing?!*

He laughed with her. "Ah, yeah, maybe we could do that." He looked as though he was about to add something, but then his face went red, and he ducked his head as he took a step back. "M-maybe I'll see you there. I should be going…" He turned and walked away.

Odd, she thought, until she too spun around to see Dane glaring. Not willing to get into an argument with him, she avoided his stare and went to grab her things. He had other ideas.

"You two were looking quite cosy over there." He was standing so close behind her she could feel him breathing down her neck. He had a wicked jealous streak, a temper too. She had found that out the hard way one night in town. They hadn't been together long, maybe three months, and had gone out with a group of friends. She had run into a friend who she hadn't seen in a few years, who also happened to be a good-looking guy. A good-looking *gay* guy, who was rather affectionate and wrapped her in a big bear hug, planting a wet kiss on the top of her head. Dane had been furious. He had ripped them apart and pushed him up against a wall, about to start throwing punches, when the bouncers stepped in. Of course, Maddi had been beside herself. She had never seen him flip out like that before, and over something so innocent at that. He had apologised and told her it would never happen again, it was just hard for him to trust after what Sacha had done to him. In the end, she had let it slide. She was not about to throw Ricki under the bus to face the wrath of Dane. She turned towards him.

"Baby," she crooned as she placed a hand on his chest, "are you a little jealous? We were just dancing. That's all." She batted her lashes, a move that always worked. "You have nothing to worry about." Sliding her hand up and around his neck, she pulled him in for a kiss.

Over his shoulder, she could see Ricki quickly turn away and walk out the door.

Chapter 3

"What do ya think? The red or the blue?" Maddi held up two dresses for Rory to see.

"Hmmm… I think the blue, it really brings out your eyes." She batted her eyes, laughing as Maddi threw a soft toy at her head. "No really, the blue is bangin', you should totally wear it."

"Blue it is then," she said as she slipped it over her head. "I don't even know why I'm so anxious, he probably won't even show." She added a necklace and some chunky bracelets.

"Which one? Dane or Ricki?" Rory teased. Maddi had given her a run-down of what had happened the night before—the chemistry with Ricki, the tension with Dane. She didn't want to hurt Dane, but lately he had been getting on her nerves, his anger towards Sacha was getting worse every day and, quite frankly, she was sick of dealing with his tantrums. She had been putting up with it because she thought it would be easier than handling the fall out—she had seen first-hand the way he was with Sacha. But now that she had met Ricki, she found she couldn't get him out of her head. There was something so appealing about him, and not just the way he moved.

"Smart arse. You know who I'm talking about." She slumped down on the couch next to Rory. "Oh, everything is so messed up. What am I going to do?" She buried her head in her friend's shoulder.

"What you're going to do is sort out if you want to be with Dane or not. Ricki shouldn't factor into it. You either wanna be with Dane, or you don't. And I'm pretty sure you don't."

"It's not that simple."

"I think it is. Don't overthink it. I've listened to you complain about how he doesn't show you any respect, keeps undermining you, and how he tries to intimidate you. I know there have been some good times, but from where I'm standing, the bad outweighs the good by far." She stroked Maddi's hair. "You deserve way better than him. I wish you could see how awesome you are, so you wouldn't let him treat you the way he does."

"Aww, you're sweet, hon. Maybe you're right." She hugged her friend tight.

"You know I am. If you were truly happy with Dane, Ricki wouldn't even be on your radar."

"Hmmm, I guess that makes sense." She sat in thought for a moment. Rory did have a point. If Dane truly made her happy then she wouldn't have even noticed Ricki. It seemed to be that Dane was more interested in getting back at Sacha than working on their relationship. Not to mention his little power play the night before. Perhaps a break was what they really needed to get some perspective. This fixation with Ricki could all be because she was frustrated with her own relationship and where it was going. How to bring it up with Dane though? It would have to wait for another night. She could hardly tell him she wanted a break when they were out socialising with friends. It could wait until tomorrow. At least it would give her the time to come up with what she would say.

"Right, enough of this moping, we have to finish getting ready. What're you wearing?" She stood up, dragging Rory with her.

"What? You don't like my trackies?" She pouted, heading for the dresser. "Fine, I guess I'll wear those cute jeans I bought then."

They were the first to get to Feeney's (just like every other week), so chose a table to stow their bags and jackets, then headed for the bar. It was always nice to get there before the crowds and have the dancefloor to themselves for a while. Rory wasn't a salsa dancer, but she could shake it with the best of them. Living with Maddi meant that she knew all the other dancers too and was happy to tag along for a few drinks. Plus, there was the added bonus of getting to scope out the guys. There's something about watching a guy who can dance, the way they are in control, the way their hips move… There was only one word for it: hot.

Sipping their vodka and Red Bull concoctions, they made their way back to the table. A few more people had started to arrive. Maddi recognised the bubbly brunette from her class, and her friend Piper. They waved excitedly.

"Ooh looks like you have some fans," Rory commented as they took a seat.

"Yeah, looks that way." Maddi smiled, "They come to my classes. Actually, it was the brunette, Charlotte, I think her name is, who convinced me to teach." She reached into her shoe bag, pulling out a strappy, silver pair of heels. "So, are you ready to get your dance on?" She winked at her friend as she quickly pulled them on.

"You know it!" Rory grinned. She may not be a dancer, but she knew how to have a good time. The music hadn't changed to salsa yet, so they were dancing *old school* as Maddi liked to call it—the kind of dancing she did before; pub dancing. They were the only ones on the floor, but it didn't bother either of them, dancing was their stress relief. It was the only time Maddi truly felt relaxed.

They had worked up quite a sweat by the time the hordes of people came in. The salsa beats were blasting now, and the floor was slowly filling up. Breathless, the girls went back to their table for a break. Dane was there with a few other dancers. He gave Maddi a brief kiss on the cheek before heading for the bar. They quite often came out by themselves to social occasions. It was nice to have a break from the constant training, and now with the classes they taught, there wasn't a lot of down time. She loved having the opportunity to dance with others and keep on her toes—she knew Dane's moves so well that she never missed a step, and dancing with different people was more challenging.

As she took her seat at the table, a familiar couple caught her eye. Sacha and Jessie were sitting at one of the corner tables.

Oh no, not tonight. This is going to cause a drama that I really can't be bothered with.

She looked around for Dane to see if he had noticed his ex. Judging by the steely look in his eyes and the way his jaw was set, he had.

Maddi slinked over to him, wrapping an arm around his. "Baby, come on, we don't have to do this. Just leave it, okay? We're here to have a good time. Save it for the comps." She attempted to pull him onto the dancefloor, but his muscles were taut with anger, and she couldn't move him.

"She shouldn't be here."

"You can't stop her from coming. It's a public place, Dane."

"Doesn't matter, she knows that we come here. It's our turf."

"Come on, let's just have a dance. Forget about them." She attempted to drag him away again, but his feet remained planted, and his eyes were locked on Sacha's.

Maddi gave up trying to reason with him and went back to Rory.

"Looks like trouble's a-brewing. You okay?" she asked.

"Yeah, I'm fine, just Dane is livid. He's going to do something stupid, I just know it."

"Ah let him, you can't control him. Let's go dance and forget him." She grabbed Maddi's hand and led her away. "Come on, shake that booty! You know you want to." She wiggled her bottom at Maddi, making her laugh. "That's more like it! Now shake it!" Rory flicked her head about to the beat, her blonde and purple streaks catching in the flashing lights. For such a petite girl, she could really throw herself about the floor. Giving in, Maddi let the music take control of her body too.

The peace only lasted for one song. Sacha and Jessie had taken to the floor and were creating quite a commotion. A circle was formed around the couple as they used showy lifts and combos.

Wow, she is a piece of work. Now I see why she and Dane worked so well together.

Maddi attempted to ignore them, but it was near impossible. A hand gripped her wrist and yanked her towards the centre of the floor. It was Dane. There was a fire in his eyes, but it wasn't directed at her. It was all for Sacha's benefit.

He couldn't take his eyes of Sacha. Every move she made, he matched. Maddi was being thrown around like a ragdoll, it was both exhilarating and humiliating at the same time. He was so angry, more so than usual. His holds were getting tighter, his fingers digging into her flesh. She wanted desperately to stop but she couldn't break free. The moves were becoming more and more daring, and the crowd loved every minute of it, cheering loudly.

Only a little bit longer and the song will end, hold on, Maddi, you can do this.

She knew it was coming, the song was building to a finish. Where was he going to go with this? A big dip?

A lift? Either way she was prepared, and then she was going to walk away. She was *not* going to get in the middle of the power struggle between those two. Not anymore. Both so desperate to be *number one* and loved by everyone.

Here it comes… and she was being thrown over his shoulder into a lift similar to that of *Dirty Dancing*. The other dancers went crazy. A thunder of clapping and cheering assaulted their ears as they panted, holding position. Maddi glanced towards Sacha to see them in a similar hold. She was glaring at Dane, and Maddi had no doubt he was doing the same. Angry that they had dragged her into their battle, she slid down Dane's back and began searching for Rory. Hot tears threatened to fall as she fought her way through the throngs of people. Bodies were pressed so close she was starting to feel faint, and then a hand grasped hers and she let herself be led outside. When they broke through, she was surprised to see that it was Ricki who had come to her rescue.

"Hey," he said shyly. "You looked like you needed to get out, I hope you don't mind."

"Uh, yeah, it was getting a bit tight in there. I get a little claustrophobic in crowds." The lie rolled right off her tongue, and he seemed to accept it. Perhaps he hadn't witnessed the whole debacle. "Thanks." She smiled at him as she realised he still had her hand in his. He must've noticed at the same time because he let his hand drop.

"Yeah, sure, no problem."

"There you are! I thought I'd lost you." Rory ran up to them, holding Maddi by the shoulders, "Are you okay?" She searched her eyes then continued on. "He's such a jerk. I can't believe he did that to you." She shook her head, rolling her sleeves up to her elbows. "You were amazing though." She nudged her then stopped when she noticed Ricki standing nervously by Maddi's side.

"Oh, Rory, this is Ricki, he saved me from the stampede. Ricki, this is my best friend, Rory."

"Hey."

"Hey yourself." She looked him up and down. *Nice* she mouthed at Maddi when his back was turned. It was a struggle to keep a straight face. "So anyways, are you okay? You looked a little pissed when you left."

"Yeah, I was. God, he was being such a dick. I've never been so humiliated in all my life." She raised her shaking hands. "He was hurting me. He's never done that before, but… I'll be surprised if I don't have bruises tomorrow."

Ricki lifted his head. "He hurt you? Let me see." He held her hands ever so gently, turning them over to see the red marks Dane had left on her. "I don't care how angry you are, you don't take it out on your girlfriend. Do you want me to say something to him?"

Whatever Maddi was expecting, it was not that. Was this the same shy guy she met the other night? Offering to defend her honour?

"Oh, no, it's okay, I can handle Dane. Thanks though." Smiling, she slipped her hands from his, their eyes locking.

"So…" Rory interrupted their moment, "You're a dancer too, huh? You certainly made an impression on this one." She pointed her thumb in Maddi's direction, grinning.

"Don't listen to her, she was dropped as a baby," Maddi said, while Rory feigned shock.

"How rude!" Laughing, she linked her arm through Maddi's. "No really, like, you like dancing with her? I'm trying to convince her to give Dane the flick." She winked at Ricki conspiratorially.

"Oh, come on, give the guy a break. He's only danced with me once. You don't have to answer, Ricki." She came to his rescue. Tempted as she was to hear what he had to say, she didn't want to pressure him. There was plenty of time for them to get to know each other first.

Chapter 4

"Are you seriously not going to talk to me?" Dane asked, frustrated. It had been three days since the showdown in town, and Maddi had barely said more than two words to him. She was still upset at the way he had acted.

"I don't know what you want me to say, Dane." She sighed as she continued to sort through her wardrobe. Anything to avoid looking him in the eye.

"I just… I just want us to be okay. Please talk to me, or yell at me if you need to. Just don't shut me out." He sounded desperate, and Maddi could feel herself giving in. She hated hearing the vulnerability in his voice. She didn't want to feel sorry for him though, he had acted like a jerk.

"You know you hurt me, right? Like physically." She pulled up her sleeve to show the marks still present on her arm. "You let your hatred take control and you took it out on me. Do you know how scary it is to be held so tight that you can't move? That you can't get away?" The shock in his eyes was obvious as he stared at the bruises on her arms. "It's horrible, Dane."

"I did that to you?" He reached for her arms, but she pulled away. His face dropped. "I'm so sorry, I didn't know. I didn't mean to. I…" His voice trailed off as he paced around the room. "I would never intentionally hurt you, you know that, right? Jesus! I'm so sorry, Maddi." He reached for her hand again, willing her to accept his apology.

"I know you didn't mean to, but you still did it. You need to get over this *thing* you have for Sacha or it's going to take over your life. It's not healthy."

"I know. I can't seem to control it, every time I see her, I see red." He paused before adding, "I'll try harder, Maddi. Really, I will, as long as you're by my side, I know I can deal with it." His eyes pleaded with her. "Please?"

Do it now. Tell him you want a break. Looking into his eyes though, she couldn't do it. She couldn't be the one to hurt him. Sighing, she agreed. "Okay, but if this happens again, I'm out. I can't take any more aggression." He pulled her in for a hug, holding her tight.

"You won't regret this, I promise."

The next evening, they were training at the studio. There was a class on, but they had gone to one of the corners to work on some moves for their routine. Maddi was still uneasy about being so close to Dane. She may have forgiven him, but she certainly hadn't forgotten what he'd done. Every time he grabbed her wrist for a lead, she couldn't help but flinch. Of course, it didn't help that the bruising was still tender. Tension was building between them, and it was making her feel even more on edge.

"You know what? I think I need a break. My arms are still a bit sore." She pulled away from him. "We can do more tomorrow, okay?" Without thinking, Dane grabbed for her, his hand landing right on top of the biggest bruise. "Ow!" she cried out as she wrenched her hand away.

"Oh shit, I'm sorry, Maddi! I didn't mean to do that. Are you okay?"

"I just told you I was still sore!" He lifted his arm to reach for her again. "Just leave me alone, okay?" She rubbed at her wrist as she started to walk towards her bag. She was fighting back tears, determined not to cry in front of everyone.

"Wait, what do you mean? It…it was an accident, Maddi."

"It's always just an accident though, isn't it?" she demanded. "I just need some time to myself, alright? Just give me some space."

"Maddi, please don't go. I wasn't thinking, it won't happen again. Baby, please."

"Actions speak louder, Dane. Just back off and give me some time. I'll call you." She turned her back and went to grab her things. Class had finished, and several people were trying to cover up that they had been watching their little tiff take place. Ducking her head, she quickly made her way out the door, trying to make sense of what had just happened.

She was so lost in her thoughts that she didn't see Ricki rounding the corner. She walked straight into him.

"Oh my God! I'm so sorry. I was away with the fairies." She looked up at him, eyes still glistening with unshed tears.

"Hey, no worries, I wasn't really watching where I was going either." He nodded to her shoe bag in hand. "Are you not coming to class?"

Was that a hint of disappointment in his voice?

"Oh, I've already been up there. I kinda had a fight with Dane so I thought I'd go for a walk and clear my head."

"Oh. Okay then." He hesitated. "Is everything okay?"

Is everything okay?

I did want a break.

"You know, I actually think it might be." She took a deep breath. "I don't suppose you feel like skipping class and joining me? Might be nice to have some company. I could even throw in a few moves, do a bit of practice with you, if you want?"

"Ah, yeah sure, why not?" He smiled warmly as she linked her arm through his.

"Excellent. Let's just walk and see where it takes us." They headed away from the studio, neither of them noticing Dane standing in the shadows, watching.

After walking for nearly an hour, they settled down for hot chocolate in a quaint little café by the river side. There were cosy nooks with cushions, well-worn couches by the fire, and a few intimate tables scattered between. They opted for one of the couches. Maddi kicked her shoes off and curled her feet underneath her.

"Ah, that feels better, those heels are gorgeous, but they are *not* made for walking in!" She laughed, her eyes shining. The fresh air and company had made her feel normal again. Unravelling her scarf and throwing it on the table beside them, she reached for the marshmallows on her plate.

"Making yourself at home, I see," Ricki joked. Maddi poked her tongue at him.

"Of course," she said matter-of-factly as she pointed at his plate. "Are you going to eat that?"

"Help yourself." He grinned as he held it out to her. Unable to help herself, Maddi grinned back. For a rough start, this was turning into a pretty good night. She felt so comfortable with Ricki, and it seemed as though the feeling was mutual now.

"So, are you still going to help me go over that move from last week?" he asked.

"Yeah, sure. We can go over whatever you want, you lead, and I'll follow." She smiled, stretching her body like a cat. "Come on, we can do it over here. There should be enough room." Jumping up and grabbing his hand, she pulled him towards the empty space.

"Here?"

"Yeah, why not? We'll give 'em a show." She winked.

"Ah, okay, I guess." He pulled her in close—careful not to touch her wrists—and began to move. She was surprised that he remembered about the bruising. They hadn't actually discussed what had taken place between her and Dane earlier. It was sweet that he cared and was being so gentle with her though. Maddi had to admit, it made her feel kind of special, like she was a fragile bird he had to protect.

She knew he was worried about dancing in front of strangers; his hands trembling in hers made it obvious. Giving them a squeeze, she willed him to continue. Someone turned the music up, encouraging them. As if a trigger had been pulled, his muscles loosened, movements becoming fluid, confident. He was feeling the music now and moving by instinct.

This is the dancing I want to do. Unplanned, unpolished, natural dancing. This is how it should always be.

She sighed, content to be led wherever the music would take them.

"You look how I feel right now," he whispered in her ear.

"And how is that exactly?" she asked, leaning into his chest.

"Happy… relaxed… at home."

"That's exactly how I'm feeling too. This is so… easy. Like we've done this a thousand times before." She smiled. "I like that. I like dancing with you."

"Yeah, I like it too. Maybe we could practice together sometimes? You know, if Dane doesn't mind, that is." At the mention of Dane's name, he broke contact, pulling them back to reality.

"It's not up to Dane who I dance with. I don't even know if I *want* to dance with him anymore. That's kind of what we argued about today." She paused, trying to find the words. "Dancing with Dane is hard work; it's his way or not at all. He doesn't *feel* the music like we do. It's all about the steps and the flashy moves." She looked into his eyes. "I *really* like dancing with you." His smile reached his eyes, making them crinkle in the corners.

"Come on then, let's give it another go." He spun her into him, making her laugh.

"Oh, go on then." They continued dancing and entertaining the patrons for another hour or so until Maddi's feet were aching. Reluctantly, they gathered their belongings and headed out the door together, hand in hand.

Chapter 5

Maddi skipped up the path to her door, a goofy smile plastered on her face. Ricki had walked her back to the studio and then given her a ride home from there. She had nervously said goodnight, unsure whether he would make a move or not. He hadn't. Just a quick hug before he headed on his way. To say she was disappointed was an understatement, but she understood why it had to be that way. Things were still kind of up in the air with her and Dane. She could hardly expect the guy to throw himself at her.

The lights were off inside, so Maddi moved silently through the house to her room, trying not to disturb Rory. She was a light sleeper and did *not* like to be woken. Maddi's room was at the other end of the house and looked out over the backyard. Pulling her curtains closed, she grabbed some clean pyjamas from her drawer and headed for the bathroom. Her phone vibrated in her pocket. Looking at the screen, she saw Dane's name come up. Not ready to talk to him yet, she hit 'ignore' and left it on her nightstand.

A glass of water, teeth brushed, pyjamas on. Maddi padded back to her room. She picked up her phone and saw six missed calls from Dane.

"Extreme," she whispered to herself, climbing into bed. She switched off her bedside lamp, and a figure appeared outside her bedroom window. She screamed then clamped her hand over her mouth.

What do I do? What do I do?

Her heart was pounding in her ears.

Get up, get up, get up!

She threw her sheets back and crept over to the window. Taking a deep breath, she ripped the curtains open. Dane was standing outside, not moving, just staring back at her, his eyes dark and menacing.

"What the fuck, Dane?! Are you out of your mind? You scared the shit out of me!" she yelled, forgetting about her sleeping flatmate.

He studied her face with a scowl. "Is he here?"

"What? Is who here?" Maddi asked, confused.

"You know exactly who I'm talking about. The guy you've spent all night with."

"Excuse me?"

"Cut the crap, Maddi. I saw you with him outside the studio."

"You've been following me? What's wrong with you? I'm allowed to have friends outside of you, Dane!" Guilt swam through her veins as she said it, knowing full well she'd wanted more with Ricki. She took a calming breath. "Go home. I'm not talking to you like this." She pulled the curtains closed and turned her back to the window. Her phone began to vibrate again. Walking slowly towards it, she saw Dane's name flashing, and anger leapt to the forefront once again. She stabbed a finger at the button and held it to her ear. In a calm but stern voice, she said, "I told you, go home. It's late."

"I just want to talk to you, Maddi. I'm going to keep ringing and banging on the door until you talk to me," he threatened.

"That's really mature. This is crazy, Dane. I don't want to talk to you right now, so please, just go." She hung up on him and switched her phone off.

"Is everything okay, hon?" Rory asked, pulling on her robe.

"Oh shit, I'm sorry, I didn't mean to wake you." She was pacing, her body shaking from adrenaline. The landline began to ring. Maddi looked at her friend, "Don't answer it, it's Dane."

"Okay… This sounds interesting. Since I'm up, you want a hot chocolate?"

"Yeah, actually that sounds good. I don't think I'm going to be getting much sleep tonight."

After a restless night, Maddi had come to the conclusion that Dane was out of control. The harassment had lasted for quite some time. In the end, Rory had had enough and threatened to call the cops. He'd left after that, though his text messages remained constant throughout the night. When Maddi switched her phone on in the morning she had been bombarded with messages:

Dane: *I just want to talk.*
Dane: *Please call me.*
Dane: *I love you, Maddi, take me back.*

Dane: *You can't do this to me! Talk to me!*

Dane: *Or maybe you're too busy with your new boyfriend. Is that it? Talk to me damn it!*

Dane: *I'm sorry, baby. I love you. Call me.*

Dane: *Please?*

Dane: *TALK TO ME!!!!!!!!!*

She had to admit, it was a little scary. She hadn't seen this side of him before. It made her wonder what really happened with Sacha and what he was really capable of. Would he hurt her? *Seriously* hurt her? Something had to be done before it was too late.

Grabbing her bag, she made her way to Dane's place. She left a note for Rory, letting her know where she was… just in case. She wanted to believe that he would be calm, but after last night, she wasn't going to take any chances.

When he came to the door, it was obvious he hadn't slept. He was wearing the same clothes as the night before, his eyes were bloodshot, his hair a mess.

"Maddi! You came! Thank God!" His eyes darted around, checking to see if she was alone. He reached for her. She took a step back. "You still think I'm going to hurt you?" he asked, disappointment evident in his eyes.

"Dane, you really scared me last night. It's not okay what you did, you know that, right? Following me, showing up at my house…" She let her voice trail off. There was a flicker of anger in his eyes, and she took a step back. "I just came to make sure you were okay. I care about you, but I meant what I said. I need some space to work things out. I think we both do."

"Don't tell me what I need! I know what I need, and it's you!"

Maddi sighed, running her hand through her hair. "I'm sorry, Dane. I just don't know what I want anymore. Things have gotten out of control. You're not the guy I thought you were and to be honest, it's kinda scary."

"Don't bullshit me. I know what you *really* want. You want to toss me aside so you can get it on with *him*," he spat at her, suddenly disgusted.

"Believe what you want to, Dane. All I'm saying is that I need a break. No contact. For a week at least, so that I can clear my head and work out what I want."

"What about what I want?" He was trying a different tact now, almost whispering and reaching for her hands again. "Doesn't it matter what I want?"

"Of course it matters, Dane, but you can't force me to stay with you."

"What about our dancing? How will we practice if I can't contact you? We've got the comps…"

"Well… I've got to think about that too. I'm not sure if dancing with you is such a good idea for me. I feel like we both want different things out of it. This business with Sacha is just too much for me to deal with."

"I told you I'm working hard to be better at handling it. I know last night things got a bit crazy, but it's just cos I love you so much. You know that, right? That I love you?"

"Yeah, I do," she whispered. "But it's not enough."

"What more can I do? I need you, Maddi."

This was harder than she thought it would be. Fighting back tears, she turned to walk away.

"I'm sorry, Dane. I just need some time."

He grabbed for her arm, swinging her back to face him. "You don't get to come here and call all the shots and then just walk away! I need you to tell me what you want. You have to choose. Me or him, Maddi? Who's it going to be? The champion dancer or the beginner? You know we could win again. We *will* win. Just pick me!" A mix of anger and desperation in his voice. "Me or him? Just answer and then you can leave." He was crowding her, blocking her path with his arms.

"You're not listening to me! I don't even care about winning anymore. I just want to dance!" She took a breath, meeting his eyes. "If this is how it has to be, and you won't give me the week, then my answer is him." She turned and strode down the drive, trying to get as much distance between them as she could.

Chapter 6

Dane couldn't believe what had just happened.

Surely she doesn't mean that? She doesn't really want to end it with me. She can't. We're meant to be together. I just need to make her see that.

He grabbed his coat and, pulling the door closed behind him, he began to walk.

With no real plan in mind, he found himself heading for the studio. No one would be there at this time of day so he would have the place to himself with no distractions. Once inside, he walked slowly around the room, looking at the trophies and medals the studio had won over the years. He studied the picture of Maddi and him, taken last year, holding their own medals with pride.

He remembered how she had grabbed his hand and kissed him that night. He hadn't expected it at all, but it had felt so right. She had the softest lips, and when she smiled … she took his breath away. If he was honest, she was well out of his league, with her clear blue eyes and drop-dead gorgeous smile, she could have any guy she desired. For a brief moment there, it had been him. And now, he may never get to feel the warmth of her kiss again. The anger slowly built up inside at the thought of not having her in his life. She was the best thing to happen to him, and he had ruined it.

No, *he* had ruined it. If *he* hadn't been involved, she never would have left.

Dane now knew why he had ended up at the studio. All the records of the dancers were stored in the office.

Yes, that's what I'll do. I'll sort him out, man to man. What was his name again? Robbie? Ronnie?

Rifling through the files, he finally came across the one he was after.

"Ricki Macavoy. That's gotta be him. I think I might just pay him a little visit." He scrawled the address down on a piece of paper and shoved it in his pocket. Haphazardly throwing the files together on the desk, he made his way out the door.

"Ricki? You there?" Dane called out as he thumped on his front door. "Ricki!" He stalked around the side of the house, checking for his car. It was still sitting in the driveway. "Come on, man, I know you're in there!" He pounded on the door again, peering through the window. He heard footsteps approaching, and the door swung open.

"Dane?" Ricki glanced side-to-side. "What's up? Is everything okay?"

"Yeah, man, of course. My girlfriend just told me she doesn't want to be with me anymore and she wants to dance with you. So, yeah, everything's fucking fantastic." He raked his hand through his hair as he glared at Ricki.

"Oh… ah… sorry? I guess if that's what she wants…"

"It's what she *thinks* she wants. You must've put it in her head. What did you say to her?"

"I didn't *say* anything. We just talked. That's all. She was upset. You really hurt her, man. She deserves to be treated better."

"And you would know, huh?"

"I know I would never hurt her like you did. Only a coward takes his anger out on the one he loves. She's way too good for you." There was a flicker of pain in Dane's eyes.

"She loves me, and I love her. We're meant to be together," he whispered, as if trying to convince himself.

"I thought you just said…" Dane pushed Ricki up against the wall before he could finish.

"*She's mine.* You got it? I don't want you sniffing around thinking you can score, cos she's going to be with me. Back off, alright?" He was in Ricki's face, breathing heavily, spit glistening on his lips. A manic look in his eyes. Ricki held his hands up to placate him. He spoke calmly.

"I wasn't trying to steal her away, Dane. Like I said, we were just talking. We're just friends."

"It better stay that way then." With one final shove, Dane let him go. "I'll be watching you." He continued to stare as he slowly backed off the porch and strode down the drive.

"Pick up, pick up, pick up!" Ricki had been trying to reach Maddi since Dane had left. It worried him that she wasn't answering her phone. Dane had been acting crazy, but surely he wouldn't have done anything stupid. Would he? There was no way he could have made it to her place on foot by now, but Ricki wasn't taking any chances. He had to see her, and it had to be now. He couldn't bear the thought of her being hurt again. Tucking his phone in his back pocket, he rounded the corner to her house.

"Ricki, hi." Maddi smiled as she answered the door. "This is a surprise."

"Sorry to just show up, you weren't answering your phone, and I was worried that something might've happened to you." He looked up at her. "Are you okay? He hasn't hurt you?" Maddi groaned.

"Oh no. My phone was charging in the other room. I didn't hear it. Sorry to worry you like that." She paused. "I take it you've seen Dane then?" Ricki nodded. "God. He just won't leave things alone." She rubbed at her face. "I'm so sorry you've been dragged into all this." She stepped aside. "You should probably come in and I'll fill you in on everything." Closing the door, she led him to the kitchen where Rory was making coffee. "Better make another cup." She smiled at her friend.

"Ah, let me guess, the cray cray has come visiting you too?" She grinned at Ricki, her brow raised in question.

"Yeah, you could say that."

"You should've been here last night. That boy's not right in the head." She handed him a steaming cup. "Milk and two?"

"Yeah, perfect. What happened last night?" he asked, full of concern.

"Long story short, he saw us talking outside the studio and followed us. He was waiting for me when I got home."

"Yeah, but in a creepy way; you missed out the part where he was standing outside your bedroom window. What a perv!" Rory added.

"Firstly, what part of that isn't creepy? Secondly, he was outside your window? That's a bit stalker-like, isn't it?" He looked at Maddi as she nodded.

"Just a touch."

Ricki frowned. "Wait, I still don't understand why he came here. If he followed us, it's not like he would've seen anything. All we did was talk and dance. We did nothing wrong."

"Yeah, to you and me it would seem that way. But he gets a little jealous. Sacha, his ex, left him for his best friend last year."

"A *lot* jealous you mean. He once bailed a guy up for giving her a hug! And he was gay!"

Maddi nodded as her friend recounted the ordeal. Thinking about it now, it should have been a sign of things to come. She just never would have guessed that it could get so bad, so quick. Maddi wanted to believe the best in people and naively thought that if she was good to others, they would be good to her. Clearly that was not the case for some people.

She looked over at Ricki as he listened to Rory's tale. She was surprised he hadn't run a mile after encountering Dane; others would have. He noticed her watching and gave her a sympathetic smile.

"You've had a pretty rough go of it with him, huh?"

"You could say that. It wasn't always like this though. He used to be sweet and kind, but now his ego and obsession with his ex has taken over." She sighed. "He got it in his head that you were *with* me last night. That's why he was here. I don't know what he would've done if you had been. He's never been quite like this before." She dropped her face into her hands. "Everything is so messed up."

Ricki moved to sit next to her. "Hey, it's gonna be okay," he soothed, awkwardly patting her knee. "We'll work this out."

"Real smooth, Romeo," Rory whispered on her way past.

Ricki, confused, pulled his hand away and stood; clearly uncomfortable.

"I ah… I wasn't trying to crack onto you. I just wanted to make sure you're okay." He looked to the door. "I can go if you want. I don't want to make things difficult for you."

Maddi huffed. "How would you be making things difficult for me? You've been a great friend. It's really sweet that you wanted to check on me." She smiled up at him.

"I just… I mean, you and Dane… I don't want to be in the way. Just tell me to leave, if that's what you need me to do."

"No. That's not what I want at all. I told Dane if I had to choose," she looked into his eyes, "I choose you."

Chapter 7

Maddi didn't see Dane for the next few days, much to her relief. After Ricki had left, she and Rory had spent the day in the kitchen baking cupcakes and cookies. Rory had a flare for cooking, and it helped to keep her mind off all the dramas. Chocolate chip cookies, red velvet cupcakes complete with cream cheese frosting, and of course, the ultimate in guilty pleasures—a huge chocolate mud cake with ganache. Aprons dusted with flour, the girls sat back to admire their hard work.

"Thanks, chick, I really needed the distraction," Maddi said as she swiped a cupcake off the counter and swiftly took a large bite. "These are fantastic," she mumbled with her mouth full.

"No worries, hon, any excuse to bake, you know that." Rory grinned, also helping herself to a healthy slice of cake. "Coffee?"

"Mmmm, sounds good." She grabbed two cups down and began scooping coffee and sugar into each cup while Rory boiled the jug. "I know I shouldn't, but I'm totally having some cake next. You're a damn fine cook. You'll make someone a good wife one of these days," Maddi teased, dodging the tea towel being flicked in her direction. "You love me really." She laughed, grabbing her friend and pulling her into a hug.

"Yeah, yeah, someone's got to." Rory hugged her back. "Speaking of…" She deliberately trailed off, pulling away. "What are we going to do about Ricki?"

"What do you mean?"

"Well, it's obvious how into you he is. And you are clearly smitten by him." She poked her friend in the arm. "Don't deny it, you two are made for each other." She paused for effect. "If I have to choose, I choose you," she mimicked playfully.

"Oh, ha ha, you're hilarious," Maddi retorted.

"I know." Rory grinned, chocolate ganache over her teeth. "Seriously though, I'm just worried that he won't make any kind of move with Dane hovering in the background. You heard what he said, he didn't want to get in the way."

"Yeah, he did seem a little more awkward being around me, and who can blame him? I'm surprised he even came over after dealing with Dane's tantrum."

"The important thing is, he *did* come. You just might have to be the one to make the first move." Rory flicked frosting in Maddi's direction. "You could always cook for him. The way to a man's heart and all that."

Wiping her face and licking the frosting from her fingers, Maddi agreed. "That's not actually a bad idea. I do cook a mean roast."

After the confrontation with Ricki, Dane had needed to cool off. The anger was burning him up inside and he hated the fact that it made him feel so out of control. He had considered going to see Maddi and trying to get her to see sense but thought better of it. If he was going to win her back, he needed to keep his cool. He had already forced her to make the wrong decision once and he was not about to make the same mistake again. No, he had to play it smart this time, show her what she was missing. The hard part was going to be getting her to hear him out. What he needed was a plan, one that would give her no option but to listen.

"He just messaged me and asked me to come over tomorrow to practice." Maddi squealed with delight.

"Chill, hon, I wouldn't exactly call that a date."

"I know, I know. But he must be thinking of me though, right? That can't be a bad thing. And it's the perfect opportunity for me to cook for him," she singsonged as she danced around the room.

"Very true, just don't be upset if he doesn't do anything. I mean, you did only just break up with Dane, remember? And he seems like a decent guy—one who probably won't want to rock the boat."

"Talk about buzz kill. I thought you wanted me to 'make a move'." She held her fingers in the air as quotation marks.

"Of course I do, ya big baby. I just don't want you to get your hopes up and get hurt. I'm just looking out for you. It's part of my duties as your best friend." Rory grinned at her. "That and beating the crap outta anyone who does hurt you." She punched the cushions on the couch to make her point. Maddi giggled.

"You're such a dork."

"Yeah, but it's part of my charm. You know you love it."

"It's true, I do. What would I do without you?" she asked, her giggles turning into laughter as she watched Rory continue her torment on the upholstery. "You'll bust a seam if you're not careful. What did that cushion ever do to you?"

"It looked at me funny," she puffed, her face glowing with a sheen of sweat from her workout.

"And that is why you're my best friend. I'd rather be on your side, than against it."

"And don't you forget it." With a mischievous look in her eyes, she quickly grabbed a discarded cushion and hurled it at Maddi's head. She managed to dodge it just before it made contact.

"Right, it's on now!" she cried, as she leapt up to fend her off. "You're going down, my friend." Grabbing a cushion each, they proceeded to pummel each other until they both collapsed on the floor in fits of laughter.

Chapter 8

Maddi was so nervous getting ready for her 'date' at Ricki's place. She had changed her outfit three times, trying to get the perfect look. Something that would be sure to make him notice her as more than just friends, but in a tasteful way. She settled on her favourite pair of dark skinny jeans with ballet flats—to emphasise her long, lithe dancers' legs, topped with a baby pink singlet and black, lacy shawl. Other than a few stray curls which she clipped back, the rest of her blonde mane was left to frame her face. She added a silver locket and a dab of lip gloss to complete her look.

Twisting and turning in front of the mirror to check herself out, Maddi gave one final twirl before grabbing her purse and phone.

"Well, I'm off then. Wish me luck!" she called out to Rory on her way to the door.

"Luck!" Rory came running out of her bedroom to get a glimpse of Maddi. "Ooh someone looks flash," she sang.

"Is it too much?"

"No, you've got it perfect, hon. Just the right amount of girl-next-door meets seductress." She winked. "Go get 'em, Tiger!"

Maddi laughed. "Grrr!" She made a claw with her free hand as she pushed the door open to leave. "Oh!"

She stopped short when she saw that Dane was standing sheepishly on the doorstep, hand up, ready to knock.

"Ah, hi. You look nice," he said awkwardly. "Are you going somewhere?"

"Ah, yeah. I'm out for the day sorry. Did you want something?" She could feel Rory coming up behind her for moral support.

"I was hoping we could go for a coffee or something. Just to talk, ya know?" he stammered. Maddi hadn't seen him quite so nervous before, it was a little endearing. She shifted uncomfortably, unsure what to say to him.

"Well, you're too late," Rory jumped in. "She's on her way out, like she said." She moved to stand slightly in front of Maddi, arms folded defensively.

"Yeah, of course. Where are you going? M-maybe I could come with you? Walk you there?"

"I don't think that's a good idea."

"You'd be kind of a third wheel, if ya get my drift," Rory sneered. Dane looked at his feet then into Maddi's eyes.

"You're going to see him?" His voice broke as he tried to hold it together. The pain in his eyes was hard for Maddi to see. She hated that she was hurting him so much.

"Dane… I…" Her shoulders sagged as she let out a sigh. "Don't make this harder than it already is, okay?" she pleaded with him. "It just wasn't working for us. You know that." She paused. "For what it's worth, nothing has happened with Ricki. I don't even know if it will. We're just friends."

Rory rolled her eyes. "Don't go getting any ideas though. She told you it's over, so you have to deal with it. Give her some space, man." She held her ground in front of Maddi, ready to jump into action, if need be.

"I... I have to go now," Maddi whispered, avoiding eye contact as she made her way down the steps.

Full of anguish, Dane took a step towards her. "Maddi, please…" His voice trailed off as he watched her walk away. Dropping his head in defeat, he let her go.

It took every ounce of willpower for Maddi to keep walking and not turn back. She felt like the biggest bitch in the world. She liked to make people happy, and this was torture for her. Her lips trembled as she fought back the tears that wanted to fall.

I will not cry. I am stronger than this. Just keep walking.

By the time she had arrived at Ricki's place, the tears that threatened had dissipated, and she was back to feeling excited. The butterflies in her stomach were going crazy as she walked up to his door. She puffed out her breath before knocking politely. "Here goes nothing," she whispered to herself.

When he opened the door and smiled that beautiful smile at her, all her nerves went out the window. She couldn't explain it, but he just put her at ease. He stood back, allowing her to walk through to the hall.

"Just down the hall and to the left." He ushered her in the direction of the kitchen. "I didn't know what you needed…" He waved his hand in the air. "The kitchen is at your disposal."

"Right, well let's get started then." She clapped her hands before removing her shawl and throwing it on a chair in the corner. "Do you have a large roasting dish?" she asked while washing her hands in the sink. She set to work, seasoning the lamb leg with salt and pepper and a few sprigs of rosemary. Ricki scrubbed the potatoes, while she chopped the rest of the vegetables. They worked side by side, in a comfortable silence, as if they had been doing this forever. Once everything was in the oven and the dishes were cleared, they sat down with a drink.

"So I thought, if you want to, maybe we could get some movies to watch, ya know, after dancing and eating and stuff." He raked his hand through his hair, something Maddi had noticed him do when he was nervous. She found it adorable, like so many other traits he had.

"Yeah, sure, that sounds great." She smiled at him, trying to make him comfortable. "Did you wanna have a dance before dinner? It'll be a while before it's ready."

"Good idea." He stood up, offering her his hand. "I don't know if I can remember what you showed me the other day…"

"You'll be fine. Believe in yourself. You're better than you give yourself credit for." She moved in close, looking into his eyes. His hands shook as he wrapped them around her. "Just take a deep breath and do whatever comes to mind. I'll follow, no matter what." Exhaling, he slowly began to move. Cautiously at first, then with more confidence. He was brilliant really. Maddi was impressed with the speed at which he learned and adapted moves. He only needed to be shown once and then he made it his own. His hands were no longer shaking, but strong and steady in his lead. He guided her through lengthy combos and spins, their bodies moving as one at times. Their eyes locked on each other's.

They were interrupted by the sound of clapping. "Wow. Dude, I didn't know you could move like that. That's awesome!"

Maddi inspected the newcomer. He was shorter than Ricki, with dark brown hair spiked up at the front. His eyes were an almost yellowy green; they looked her up and down as he let out a whistle. "Damn, brother, she's a looker." He winked at her.

Laughing, Ricki made the introductions; "Maddi, this is my flatmate Damon, Damon, this is Maddi—the one I was telling you about."

"Nice to meet you, Damon. I'm interested to know what he's been saying about me." She grinned, offering her hand for him to shake.

"All good, I promise you." He chuckled. "Is it you who's responsible for those delicious aromas coming from the kitchen?" He took a deep breath in through his nose. "My stomach's grumbling just smelling it."

"Guilty. I hope you like roast lamb and lots of veggies." She couldn't help but grin at him.

"She cooks, she dances, and she's smokin'—if you don't mind me saying—she's a keeper." He winked at her again.

Maddi laughed. "Thanks, I like to think so." She was distracted by the sound of her phone ringing. "Excuse me, I'd better go see who that is." She jogged into the kitchen where she had left her things. Flashing on her screen was the name 'Dane'. She groaned, pushing the ignore button.

"Everything okay?" Ricki asked when he saw her face as she walked back in.

"Yeah, it's just Dane. I don't feel like dealing with him right now."

"Has he been hassling you again?"

"No, not really. He made an appearance this morning, asking me to go for a coffee to 'talk'. I was on my way over here though, so…" She gave him a shy smile. "I turned him down of course. Rory couldn't wait to tell him that I was coming over here for the day." As if on cue, her phone buzzed again. Having a quick glance at it, she put her phone aside once more.

"He's persistent, I'll give him that. I take it he's the ex?" Damon asked, stretching out on the couch.

"Yep, that's him. He doesn't seem to understand the concept of giving someone space." She wrinkled her nose. "Anyways, I should check on dinner. It should be ready soon." She busied herself in the kitchen, turning the vegetables, basting the lamb, all the while ignoring the buzzing that went off every few minutes. Ricki could see how agitated she was getting.

"Hey, do you want me to answer it? I can tell him to give it a break, see if that helps?" His offer was sweet. Maddi wasn't sure it would work, but she didn't really know what else to do to get through to him.

"Thanks. That might at least get him to stop for today." She handed her phone over, their fingertips brushing lightly, sending a shiver up her arm. "Hey." She reached out. "I'm really sorry you've gotten stuck in the middle of this. I… I really appreciate you being here with me." She leaned in to give him a quick peck on the cheek, making him blush.

"Anytime you need me, I'll be here." He gave her hand a gentle squeeze. "I'd better answer this, put him out of his misery." He held the phone to his ear. "Dane, it's Ricki… No, she doesn't want to talk to you right now… I understand, man, but she just wants to relax for the day without any stresses, ya know? I know you want to talk to her, but you have to give her some space… I don't think that's any of your business… No… We're friends, hanging out, dancing and eating, no big deal… Look, man, you have to let it go. She'll talk to you when she's ready, but it's not going to be today… I'm hanging up now." He pushed the end button and handed the phone back to Maddi. "I don't know how much good it did."

"Thanks for trying anyways." She switched her phone to silent and put it under her shawl. "Out of sight, out of mind." She attempted a smile. "You hungry?"

"You bet." Ricki retrieved the plates from the cupboard and called out to Damon, "Grubs up!"

"Finally! I'm starving in here!" He came running into the kitchen. "Mmmm, smells good. You can come visit anytime you like, Maddi." He swung an arm around her shoulders playfully.

"Be careful what you wish for, I just may take you up on that." She beamed as she dished up a huge plateful of food for him. Lamb, roast potatoes, pumpkin and kumara, along with peas and corn smothered in gravy. The boys were in heaven.

"It's so good," Damon murmured between mouthfuls. "So, so good."

"It really is. I haven't had a meal like this since I left home. I'm with Damon, you can totally cook for us anytime you like," Ricki said, scraping the last of what was on his plate, onto his fork.

"Aww, thanks guys. I'm glad you like it." She smiled contentedly. "Maybe we could do this every week," she suggested.

"I'm totally down with that," Damon said, "Seriously, man, you gotta put a ring on this one. If you don't, I will." He nudged Ricki, chuckling. "I'll take care of the dishes tonight. Leave you two in peace." He gathered up the empty plates and made his way to the kitchen.

Chapter 9

After filling their stomachs, Maddi and Ricki took a stroll to the local DVD store to hire out some movies. The sky was just beginning to darken, and the air was a little crisp, but it felt good to be out. Maddi had checked her phone before leaving and discovered several more missed calls and text messages. Did he not realise how much stress he was putting her under? How much he was pushing her away? All she wanted was to be free from dramas, even if for just one day. Was that too much to ask?

"You okay? You seem far away," Ricki asked, studying her face. Turmoil weighed heavily on her shoulders, and it showed in her eyes. "We don't have to get movies if you don't want to, we can just talk or whatever. Up to you."

Maddi gave a tight smile. "No, a movie is just what I need." She gave him a sidewards glance. "Just promise me, no love stories."

"Aww really? I was so hoping for a good romance," Ricki joked, jostling her with his elbow.

"I knew it! You're a big softy." She latched onto his arm, "You're just a big teddy bear inside, aren't you?"

"Hey, I can be manly when I need to be." He puffed his chest out, strutting like those body builders whose muscles are too big for their bodies. Maddi laughed as she watched him strike a pose in the middle of the street.

"Oh wow, that's super manly." She giggled, once more grabbing his arm and dragging him along the path towards the store.

"Anything to hear that laugh." He looked down at her, his eyes crinkling in the corners as he smiled. She lifted her face to meet his gaze. They were close enough that she could feel the heat radiating from his body. She let out an involuntary shiver.

"Are you cold? Do you want my jacket?"

"Then *you* would be cold. We're almost there, I'm okay." She slipped her hand into his and put it in his jacket pocket, their arms pushed up against each other. "This will keep me warm enough until then."

Once they had selected their movies and made their way back to his flat, Ricki set about making popcorn and grabbing blankets to keep them cosy. The curtains were pulled to keep in what little heat was left in the room. Maddi curled up on the couch, a blanket draped over her legs as she waited for the movie to begin. Ricki sat down next to her.

"Ready?" he asked, fingers poised over the remote control.

"Almost," she said as she sidled in closer. "It's a little chilly, I hope you don't mind." She swung her legs over his lap and leaned her head on his shoulder, pulling the blanket tight around them both. Ricki wrapped his arm around her shoulder.

"Not at all. This is nice." He pressed the button to start the DVD and rested his free hand on her leg. Maddi found it hard to concentrate on anything other than the closeness of their bodies and the smell of his cologne. The realisation that she was within kissing distance made her heart hammer in her chest and her mouth go dry. She tried her best to focus on the film.

"Don't mind me, I'm just going to pick at the leftovers," Damon said as he strolled past. "You guys want anything from the kitchen?"

"A water would be great, thanks," Maddi answered, lifting her head, "Oh and the popcorn! We left it on the bench." She resumed her position, snuggling just a little bit closer still.

There was rustling from the other room, and then quiet voices. Footsteps and then a clearing of the throat.

"Ah, guys? You have a visitor." Damon stood sheepishly in the doorway, with a grief-stricken Dane beside him. His eyes were darting back and forth between Maddi and Ricki, taking in the scene before him.

"I… I just want to talk to you, Maddi, you weren't answering your phone. Can we go somewhere? Please?"

"Oh my God, Dane." Maddi swung her legs from Ricki's lap. "I wasn't answering my phone for a reason. I already told you, I don't want to talk to you. Not today." She waved her hand towards Ricki. "I know Ricki told you too." She folded her arms across her chest. "Showing up here isn't exactly doing you any favours." Her voice shook with wariness as she massaged her temples. "I'm not going anywhere with you, so you may as well leave."

Damon stepped aside with a nod of his head. "I'll show you out then."

"No, I don't want to go yet. I just got here and I'm not leaving until she speaks to me. She owes me that much." He pointed an accusatory finger at her.

Damon placed a hand to Dane's chest. "Mate, this isn't your house. You don't get to decide who stays and who goes. Maddi is our guest, and she clearly doesn't wanna see you, so I suggest you make this easy and leave."

Dane looked down at the hand on his chest then up to meet Damon's eyes. He squared his shoulders, his fists held at his side.

"Guys, stop." Maddi stood up. "There's no need for this. Dane, you have five minutes to say your piece and then you have to go. No more calls, no more texts. I'm done. Okay?" She touched her hand to Damon's chest, holding him back. "Thanks." She smiled.

"Is that a good idea, Maddi? Do you want me to come with you?" Ricki asked gently.

"It's okay, Ricki, thanks. Dane won't hurt me, will you?" she asked, touching his arm to draw his attention away from Damon.

"Of course I won't hurt you! I've apologised for that, and I swear it'll never happen again." He raked a hand through his dishevelled hair. "I just want to talk."

"Damn right it won't happen again. Five minutes and then I'm coming to get her, and you will get off my property." Ricki spoke evenly, holding his hand up, palm out. "Five minutes," he said again.

"I'll be okay," she soothed, "I'll be back soon, you go get the popcorn ready." She forced a smile, trying desperately to calm the situation. A fight was the last thing she wanted. Everything seemed to be escalating out of control. She grabbed Dane by the arm and pulled him to the door. "This better be good," she muttered.

Outside, Maddi stood on the step above, staring blankly at Dane. For someone who only had a brief time allowance, he didn't seem to be doing much talking. He paced back and forth, stopping to look at her before beginning again.

"I thought you wanted to talk?"

"I thought you said nothing was going on with you two?" he finally said.

Sighing, Maddi responded, enunciating every syllable to ensure that it sank in this time. "For the last time, Dane, nothing is going on with *us*," she pointed between the two of them for emphasis, "or with me and Ricki, *not* that it's any of your business. What you saw in there, was two friends watching a movie together. It's cold. I cuddled in for body heat. Oooh big deal." Sarcasm dripped from her lips as she waved her hands in the air.

"Okay, okay." He held his palm up to calm her. "You just looked so cosy, and I miss that. It used to be me that kept you warm. It seems like you've moved on straight away and I meant nothing to you." His eyes glistened with tears.

"Don't you dare try to lay the guilt on me. I've done nothing wrong here." She pointed a finger at his chest. "*You* were the one who was obsessed with Sacha, *you* were the one who used me to get to her and bruised my arms at the same time, *you* were the one who followed me home and harassed me." Her voice was rising with every point she made. "And then you have the audacity to show up here, after being told to leave me alone, and try to ruin my night! Didn't anyone ever tell you, no means no?"

"Maddi, please, I know it's my fault. And I'm sorry. You know I can't think straight around you though. This isn't what I wanted to happen." He dropped his head in his hands.

"Oh really? Tell me, *Dane*, what did you think would happen? Huh? Did you think I'd come running back into your arms because you showed up? Or were you hoping to catch me doing something so that you would have an excuse to start a fight?"

"No! That's not what I want… I just… I don't know! I just went crazy when you wouldn't talk to me, so I had to see you. We were good together once. I miss you." He reached for her hands, begging her, a tear spilling over.

She pulled away from him. "Don't. Touch. Me," she seethed.

The door opened behind her, making her jump. "It's been five minutes. You want me to get rid of him?" Ricki stood in the doorway, his body rigid, hands balled into fists.

"Thanks, I think we're done here." She looked at Dane "You can leave now." Folding her arms, she stood her ground, waiting for him to move. His body sagged in defeat. With one last look at them, he turned on his heel and slowly loped down the drive.

When she could no longer see him, Maddi twisted around to face Ricki. He hadn't moved except to look down at her. She brushed her fingers lightly over his fists and up his arms, feeling each part relax with her touch. When she reached his shoulders, she stepped towards him, leaning her head against his chest. He wrapped his arms around her, cradling her as she cried.

"Sorry." She sniffed, her voice muffled in his shirt. "I didn't realise how angry I was." He stroked her head gently while the other hand slowly rubbed circles on her back. "Did you hear me screaming at him? I kinda lost control for a bit there." She looked up at him, mascara smeared under her eyes. Using his thumb, he softly wiped it away.

"He deserved all of it and more. Damon had to hold me back. It wasn't easy leaving you out here with him, knowing what he's capable of. I don't trust him, Maddi." He felt her shiver against him. "Shit, you must be freezing. Come on, let's get you back inside." He gathered her in his arms and led her back to the lounge where Damon was waiting.

"Everything okay? Do we need to break some bones?" he said, standing when he saw them enter.

Maddi smiled. "Everything's fine now, Damon. Thanks." She gave him a hug. "I can't believe you were going to jump in there for me when we've only just met."

"Purely selfish reasons I'm afraid." Maddi frowned, so he continued, "Well, I could hardly let someone hurt you after you cooked such a mean feed now, could I? Not when you've promised to do it again." He winked.

Maddi laughed, playfully whacking his arm. "I guess it's a good thing I didn't burn dinner then, eh?" She grinned. "So, are we gonna watch the rest of these movies or what?" She plonked herself down on the couch, clutching the bowl of popcorn in one hand, patting the cushion next to her with the other. "What are you waiting for?" Ricki took up his spot beside her again, while Damon lounged on one of the recliners in the corner. The corny jokes on screen had her laughing again, the tension slowly draining from her body.

Chapter 10

When Maddi awoke the next morning, she blinked slowly, taking in her surroundings. She was still on the couch in the lounge, where she must've fallen asleep during the movie. Ricki's arm was draped casually around her middle as he lay peacefully behind her. Her head was resting on his chest, and their legs were intertwined. Sighing contentedly, she snuggled in, taking full advantage of the warmth of his body. She slid her hand over his, careful not to wake him, and closed her eyes once more.

I could get used to this.

She was wearing a beautiful, flowing, white gown and she was dancing a waltz with Ricki. They were circling the dancefloor, their audience captivated. It was almost as if they were dancing on air, their movements were so fluid. He looked impeccable in his suit and tie, and she felt like a princess in his arms.

When the music came to an end, they looked into each other's eyes. He brushed his hand down her cheek, ever so softly, whispering how beautiful she was. He cupped her chin, tilting her face towards his, as he slowly lowered his lips to hers…

"Son of a bitch!" Damon came crashing into the room, waking them from their sleep. "Shit, sorry, I didn't mean to wake you. I stubbed my toe on the door. You would not believe how much it hurts!" He hopped over to the recliner.

Maddi stretched her arms above her head, hoping no one noticed her flushed cheeks. Ricki was still lying behind her but propped up on his elbow, his other hand lightly stroking her hip.

"How did you sleep?" he asked.

"Really good actually. You're quite the hot water bottle." She smiled up at him, her eyes drifting to his mouth as he smiled back.

"Oh good, glad to know I have a purpose." He chuckled. He didn't seem to be in any hurry to get up, which suited Maddi just fine. She couldn't help but think about how different he was from their first encounter. He had been so shy and quiet, barely making eye contact. Now, he lay beside her, joking around, as if it was the most normal thing in the world.

"What's the plan for today?" he asked, brushing a stray hair behind her ear.

"Ah, I hadn't really thought about it. Do you have to work?"

"Not till this afternoon. Are you teaching tonight?"

"Oh shoot. Yes, I am. I guess I'll be working on a class plan then." She flopped her head back onto the couch, her brow creased. Ricki pushed himself up and climbed over her, much to her disappointment.

"Well, I'd better get to work on your breakfast then," he said, as he made his way to the kitchen. "You can't concentrate on an empty stomach. I hope you like eggs!" he called out.

Maddi swung her legs over the side of the couch and padded to the bathroom to freshen up. Borrowing a squirt of toothpaste on her finger, she hastily 'brushed' her teeth to be rid of any morning breath. She splashed water on her face and combed her hair with her fingers. "You'll pass," she said to herself, looking in the mirror.

In the kitchen, Ricki was busy whipping up scrambled eggs on toast, and a pot of coffee was brewing. He was humming to a tune on the radio, unaware of Maddi watching. She was tempted to walk up behind him and wrap her arms around his waist but decided against it. Even though the signs were there, she still wasn't a hundred percent sure he was interested. Unlike other guys she had known, Ricki seemed content to just hang out with her as a friend. It was both refreshing and frustrating.

"Mmmm, smells good," she said, settling on standing next to him at the counter. "Anything I can do to help?" she asked, helping herself to a cup of coffee.

"Nope, all done. Here, I hope you like it." He smiled, handing her a steaming plate.

"Are those chives I see?"

"Of course. I'm not a complete dud in the kitchen, you know." He winked at her. "Damo, eggs are ready if you want 'em."

"Hells yeah!" he bellowed from the lounge. Sauntering in, stubbed toe forgotten, he grabbed a plate and joined them at the table. "Mate, you have outdone yourself." He clapped his hands before digging in. "You know, if you two get hitched, I'm totally gonna live with you, eh? You're cooking is mean." Maddi and Ricki laughed. "You think I'm joking, but I'm not. You're stuck with me forever."

After breakfast, Maddi said her goodbyes and headed back home to prepare for class. She switched her phone back on as she walked and saw a text from Rory asking how her night had been and when she would be home. She quickly scrolled through the other messages before replying. Most were from Dane before he had shown up, she was pleased to see that he hadn't bothered her again after her little temper tantrum.

Starting a new message, she clicked out a text for Rory.

Maddi: *Hey chick, great night with Ricki. He's so adorable. Fell asleep on the couch watching movies. Had a visit from Dane though! Can you believe he showed up there? How rude is he? He was calling non-stop and texting. Ricki even answered and told him to back off, it was sweet. Then he shows up when we're snuggling on the couch. I could've died! I did my nut at him, went a bit mental actually, but he makes me so angry! Anyways, I'll fill you in more when I get home. See you soon!*

"Sending to Dane" came up on the screen. "Oh shit! Oh no!"

Within seconds, her phone was buzzing in her hand. A text flashed up on the screen from Dane.

Dane: *What the fuck Maddi?*
Maddi: *Sorry, that wasn't meant for you.*
Dane: *You spent the night with him?!*
Maddi: *That's none of your business.*

She groaned in frustration. *Way to ruin a great morning, Maddi. Stupid, stupid, stupid!* She switched her phone back on to silent and hurried the rest of the way home. Rory would know what to do.

Rounding the corner, she could see Dane already on her doorstep, arguing with Rory. He must've been on his way there when she had sent the text.

"Un-fucking-believable!" she hissed to herself.

"I told you already, she's not here!" Rory's voice carried across the air.

"Don't bullshit me, Rory! She must be home by now, I know she left his place already. Maddi! *Maddi!*" he yelled, as he attempted to force his way past.

"I'm going to call the cops if you don't back off!" She shoved his chest. Maddi quickly ran up the path before it could escalate any further.

"What the fuck is going on here?" she demanded, staring Dane down. "It's bad enough you showing up last night, now you're harassing my flatmate too?"

"I'm not harassing anyone!" He held his hands up defensively.

"The fuck you're not!" Rory spat. "Coming here, trying to push your way in. You're a fucking joke!"

Dane narrowed his eyes. "You watch your mouth, little girl." He pointed his finger in her face.

"Hey! You keep away from her! This is between you and me, leave her out of this." Maddi stepped in front of her friend. "Now, I suggest you go and cool off, before I call the cops and get a restraining order on you."

"That's a little dramatic, don't you think?" He scoffed, folding his arms across his chest.

"Oh really? I've got plenty of witnesses who will testify that you're stalking me."

"You think I'm stalking you?"

"You don't? What would you call it then?" Maddi asked sarcastically.

"I keep telling you, I just want to talk. I know we could work through this if you would just hear me out."

"Do you hear yourself? You're like a broken record! You keep saying you want to talk, and then when I actually give you the chance, you don't say anything! You're trying to control me, telling me who I can and can't hang out with. You need to get it through your head—I'm not yours to control. I never was!" She took a step back, running her hand through her hair. "Please, just go, okay? I don't want to see you anymore." She felt Rory's hands holding her steady as she swayed with emotion. Determined to make her point, she forced herself to continue her cold stare. His face crumpled. He wiped at his eyes as he backed away.

"Okay. I get it," he whispered as he left. Maddi watched as he broke down when he reached the path. His sobs were destroying her. She turned to her friend and buried her face in her shoulder as she wept. Rory continued to rub her back soothingly as she led her inside and closed the door.

Chapter 11

Allowing herself some time to cry and let out all the anger and sadness she was holding in, Maddi curled up in a ball on her bed. Rory kept popping in to check on her every half hour, bringing coffee and chocolate. After two hours, she'd had enough. Something needed to be done.

"Okay, hon, I know things are shitty at the mo, but you have to pick yourself up. You have class tonight, remember? Don't you have to practice or something? You know it always makes you feel better."

Maddi sniffed. "Yeah, you're right. I don't know why I'm letting him get to me so much." Wiping her eyes, she stood. "I might get some practice in now before I have a shower. Thanks." She gave a small smile. Heading to her iPod, she caught a glimpse of herself in the mirror. Red, puffy eyes, hair dishevelled, still in last night's clothes—she looked a right mess. Ignoring her reflection, she turned on some music, and let it wash over her, cleansing away the negativity of the last few days. Her hips began to sway, her feet soon following the beat. It wasn't long before she was drenched in sweat, puffing. It felt good to be moving. Within an hour she had perfected her lesson plan for the evening and even added some new moves to her choreography.

Satisfied with her afternoon's work, she showered and dressed in a pair of black leggings with pink leg warmers and heels. Her long pink tee hung off her shoulder and she pulled her hair to the side in a messy plait. Her eyes were still a little puffy around the edges, but it was nothing a touch of makeup couldn't cover. At least she no longer resembled a zombie.

Grabbing her bag and dance shoes, she headed for Rory's room to say goodbye.

"Hey! You look much better. See? I told you dancing would help." She winked, a grin twitching at her lips.

"Thanks, I *feel* better. I've made a decision too. I'm going to try and keep things civil with Dane. I don't need all this stress, and I don't want you to be stuck in the middle of it either."

"Fair enough. You know I'll back you up, though, no matter what." She pulled Maddi in for a hug, "But if you change your mind, you just say the word and I'll kick his arse." She sprang back into a fighting pose, waving her arms through the air.

Maddi laughed. "Of course. You'll be the first to know if that happens."

Up at the studio, Maddi was busy setting up when Lisa walked in.

"Okay." She drew out the word as she glanced behind her. "I wasn't expecting you in tonight. Dane rang to cancel. Any idea why?" She folded her arms across her chest.

"Oh, ah. That's probably my fault. We broke up a few days ago." Maddi winced. "Things have been a bit tense between us," she said sheepishly. "I honestly thought he'd still come to class though, sorry. I can still do the partner work without him though, it's just his styling class that will be effected."

"I'm sorry to hear that, Maddi. If you're not up to classes, I understand if you want to cancel too."

"No, no. Really, I'm fine." She smiled to prove her point. "I'm not going to let my personal life get in the way of work. You have nothing to worry about."

"Okay, well, if you ever need to talk…" Lisa squeezed her hand, then she walked back to the desk to get ready for the students who would be arriving any minute.

Maddi turned back to her music, unsure how to feel about Dane not coming. Before she had had too much time to think about it, her students started flowing through the doors, excited babble filling the room.

"I have been waiting for this all week! I love your classes," Piper gushed.

"Yeah, totally! What are we doing tonight? I've been practicing my body rolls," Charlotte added eagerly.

"That's great, guys, I'm glad you like my class. Good to get some feedback." She winked, "You're in luck, Charlotte, body rolls make a feature in the move tonight." The two girls beamed as they took their places in the front row. Maddi called the others to attention and took them through their warm-up. She watched in the mirror, pleasantly surprised at how well the girls were moving compared to the last lesson. "Awesome, guys. I can tell you've been practicing, which is a good thing cos tonight's move is a tricky one." She quickly ran through the combo she had prepared, and then bit by bit she broke it down.

While the girls went through each part, she walked around, giving pointers where needed. "Great work. Make sure you don't roll your shoulders forward when you do your body rolls. You should feel it in your core. Are you feeling it?"

"Yes," they chorused, clearly enjoying themselves. There was a lot of chatter and laughter as they perfected their rolls.

"Alright, let's put it all together. One, two, three… five, six, seven." They rolled and shimmied to the beat, their bodies glistening with sweat by the end. "Nice work, guys. We're almost out of time, so we'll try it to the music and then you can film it to practice at home." She pushed play, and counted them in. "Five, six, seven!" She did it with them the first time, and then stepped aside to watch. Every one of them managed to pull it off, and Maddi beamed with pride.

"You guys rock! I love it! In fact, you're giving me an idea." She smiled, looking at each of them. "I've been working on a choreography for the comps which I was going to do solo, but now I'm thinking, maybe I should have a team. What do you think?" Several girls jumped up and down, their eyes wide.

"Oh my God, yes, yes, *yes*! That would be sooo cool!" Piper was the first to comment.

"Well, anyone interested, send me a text or leave your details with Lisa, and I'll organise a plan for rehearsals. It'll be a lot of work, but it'll be rewarding too."

As the girls flittered about the room or chatting with Lisa, Maddi spotted Ricki walking in. She smiled at him, beckoning him over.

"You're a sight for sore eyes. I couldn't ask a huge favour, could I?" She peered up at him, eyes pleading.

"Oh, I see how it is." He pointed a finger at her. "You don't play fair. How can I turn down that face?" He grinned.

"Oh!" She clapped her hands. "Thanks so much. Dane cancelled on me, and I need you to fill in for him."

His smile waivered.

"Just to demonstrate a move. You don't have to say anything. I'll do the talking. I just, you know, need a body to show them how it looks, and I can't do it by myself." She stood on tiptoes, pressing her hands to his chest. "Please?"

"I… ah… I guess so. Where is Dane?" he asked. "Why did he cancel?"

"Ah, long story short, I had a bit of a run in with him after I left your place this morning, I may have told him I'd get a restraining order on him," she replied awkwardly.

"Are you okay?" He studied her face, noticing the bloodshot eyes.

She nodded. "Yeah, I'm fine. I'll tell you all the details later if you want."

He pulled her in to him, wrapping his arms around her waist and resting his chin on her head. "I'm glad you're okay. We can go for a coffee after class if you want. I have no plans."

"Thanks, that would be good," she said, enjoying the warmth of his embrace. But it couldn't last. They had work to do.

Reluctantly, she pulled away. "We should probably go over that move before everyone arrives." She took his hand. "Come on."

The class went off without a hitch. Ricki had been shaking when they did the demonstration, but once that was over with, he loosened up—even offering help to the men in class. Maddi was glad she had roped him into it.

After packing up, they walked through town discussing the evening's happenings, heading for that same little café by the river. They ordered and looked for a table this time, one a bit more secluded where they could talk in private. They each draped their jackets over the backs of their chairs, talking animatedly until their drinks arrived. Maddi wrapped her cool hands around the steaming mug of hot chocolate and inhaled. The sweet smell instantly reminding her of their last visit to this place. She smiled at the memory.

"What?" Ricki grinned back at her, taking a sip of his drink and leaving a foamy moustache above his lip.

"Do I have something on my face?" he deadpanned. Maddi couldn't contain her laughter.

"No, not at all." She smirked as he wiped his mouth with a napkin. "I was just thinking about the last time we were here. It was the first time you seemed to relax with me."

He chuckled. "Yeah, I was pretty nervous when I first met you." He stretched his arms above his head, his shirt lifting slightly. "Not now though." He grinned. Maddi's eyes drifted to the section of bare skin showing under his shirt. Defined abs and a dusting of hair leading a trail under the waistband of his pants. She blinked her eyes back up to his, her cheeks colouring when she met his gaze. Busted.

Ricki shifted forward, resting his elbows on the table between them. "I don't want to distract you from the pleasantries, but you were going to tell me what happened today." Maddi was thankful for the change of direction.

"Yeah, that's right, I was." She slowly recounted the whole ordeal from the miss-sent text to the restraining order threat.

"Wow, that's pretty ballsy of you. I'm impressed. You did the right thing, though." He reached across and placed his hand over hers. "If he shows up again, you can call me, you know that, eh? Anytime of the day or night. If you need me, I'll be there." His thumb was tracing circles around her hand, making it impossible for her to concentrate. He was staring into her eyes with such intensity, she had to look away.

Should I? Shouldn't I?

Taking a deep breath, Maddi looked up at him once more. "Ricki, I… ah… I just don't know what I would do without you. I know we haven't known each other long, but I feel a connection with you that I've never felt before."

"Yeah, me too. And don't worry, I'm not going anywhere." He smiled.

"Good. Because… I was… I mean to say… um, I really… like you." She looked down at their hands and then back to his eyes. "Like, a lot."

Ricki pulled back, his brow furrowed. "I… I really like you too."

"You do?"

"I do, but I think… we're better as friends, don't you? I mean, I wouldn't want to ruin what we have."

"Oh. Okay. I understand." She bit her lip, shaking her head. "No, you're right. Why ruin a good thing, eh?" She forced a smile on her face as she sat back in her seat. Twisting her fingers in her lap, she averted her eyes. How did people do this? Put themselves out there, only to be rejected? It wasn't something she'd really had to deal with in the past, and it hurt more than she cared to admit. Tears welled in her eyes, but she fought them back, determined not to show him how much she was hurting.

"Well, I guess it's time to head home then. I've gotta plan my next lesson anyway…" She stood up, desperate to put some distance between them.

"Maddi, wait. You don't need to rush away."

"No, I'm not rushing. I'm okay. I really do have stuff to do." She offered a small smile.

"Okay then, if you're sure?" His eyes searched hers, and she nodded. He stood with her. "Are we still going to dance this week?"

"Yeah, of course. Maybe we could check out my old studio or something." She wrapped her scarf around her neck and put her jacket on. "Well, I guess I'll just text you tomorrow then." She turned and walked away, head held high, when all she really wanted to do was curl into a ball and hide.

Ricki watched her walk out the door.

I'm such an idiot.

I can't believe I just turned down the most beautiful woman I've ever known.

But how could I possibly begin to explain to her how much she means to me? I'd rather have her in my life than not, and a girl like that will always have guys after her. She'll see eventually. She's way too good for me.

Chapter 12

Maddi didn't text Ricki for a few days. She had been too embarrassed to face him again. It was Rory who had convinced her to persevere with him.

"Maybe he's just scared. He is totally into you. I can see it in his eyes, and from everything you've told me, he's definitely keen. I think you should just forget about that conversation and pretend it never happened. Who knows, maybe he's one of those guys who has to do the asking."

"I guess…" Maddi was unsure, but she didn't really have any other options if she wanted him in her life—which she did. "Okay, I'll text him and see if he wants to dance tonight."

"Good idea."

Maddi: *Hey, you wanna go dancing tonight? I thought we could try a different studio for a change.*

Ricki: *Hey yourself, I was starting to worry that you'd forgotten about me.*

Maddi: *Sorry, I've had a busy couple of days. I'm here now.*

Ricki: *Great! Name the time and place and I'll meet you there.*

Maddi: *7pm, Latin Flava.*

Ricki: *It's a date.*

Maddi smiled at his last message. She knew he didn't mean it that way, but it still made her heart skip a beat. They had so much fun when they were together, and even though she had been mortified at his reaction, she still couldn't wait to see him again. Even if it was just as friends.

Eager to see Maddi and ensure she really was okay with him, Ricki arrived at the studio ahead of time. He paced nervously outside the doors, not ready to go in alone.

Even after helping Maddi with her class the other night, he was still wary of dancing in front of others—especially a whole bunch of people he had never met before.

This was his first time at Latin Flava, and he wasn't sure what to expect. Others were milling about, nodding as they passed. He recognised a few faces from Feeney's Bar, but it didn't help his unease.

"Well, who do we have here?" Sacha drawled, chewing gum loudly and twirling a strand of dark hair around her finger. She looked him up and down with an appreciative grin.

Ricki glanced side-to-side before pointing a finger at his chest. "Ah, are you talking to me?" When she nodded, he stammered, "I… I'm Ricki." He recognised her from the bar. She was the one who had caused the friction between Dane and Maddi that night.

"Hi, Ricki, I'm Sacha," she purred, "You waitin' for someone?" She leaned in close, her minty breath assaulting his nostrils.

"Ah, yeah. Maddi. I'm waiting for Maddi." He stepped back, trying to put some distance between them. She laughed, a deep throaty laugh, and took his hand.

"What's the matter? You scared of me? I don't bite… not unless you want me to." She winked, a wicked gleam in her eye. "Come on, I'll introduce you to everyone." She dragged him through the doors, ignoring his protests.

"I really should stay outside and wait for her…"

"Oh, come on. She's a big girl. I'm sure she can find her way in. This *is* her old studio after all." Sacha threw her belongings on the table. She flicked her jet-black hair over her shoulder and pulled Ricki behind her. She had quite a strong grip for such a petite person.

After circling the room and introducing him to everyone, Sacha escorted him back to the front. She still had hold of his hand and wasn't showing any signs of letting go. Ricki was feeling more and more uncomfortable, but he didn't know how to get rid of her. Standing up to Dane was one thing, but Sacha was different. It didn't feel right to tell her to back off; she was just being friendly after all.

"Hey, you wanna have a dance?" She wiggled her hips in front of him.

"Ah, thanks, but I think I'll just wait for Maddi." He managed to squeeze his hand out of hers and take a step back.

Sacha pouted her full, red lips. "Please?" She pushed herself up against his chest. "Just one little dance?" She walked her fingers up his chest with each word she spoke, her free arm snaking around his back. She was peering up at him, her eyes wide, and her finger still caressing his chest.

"I… ah… haven't warmed up yet… so… maybe later?" he said, removing her hand and hoping she would accept his excuse.

"The dance would be a warmup, silly." She giggled playfully. Reaching up, she cupped the back of his head and pulled him closer, whispering, "You won't regret it, I promise." Her hips grinding up against him, she slowly moved to look him in the eyes, her mouth grazing his jaw. Licking her lips, she leaned in, tilting her head up.

Panic set in.

"Woah!" Ricki pulled out of her grip. He glanced up, seeing Maddi standing in the doorway, her mouth dropped open and eyes glistening with tears. She quickly turned on her heel and strode out of the studio before he could stop her.

"What the hell was that?" he demanded of Sacha.

"What? Just a friendly peck." She grinned impishly as she watched Maddi disappear. "Oops. Are you two, ya know? Together?" She held her hand to her mouth, feigning guilt.

"That's none of your business, Sacha. Stay away from me," he seethed, gathering his gear as he ran out the door.

Maddi couldn't believe her eyes. This certainly wasn't what she expected when she organised for them to meet at her old studio. If she had known Sacha would be there, she never would have suggested it. And now, here she was, watching Sacha fawn all over the man she had feelings for. Clearly he was quite taken by her too. She was draped across him, holding him close, and he certainly wasn't pulling away.

Is that why he doesn't want to be with me?
Why does it have to be her?
What is it about her that drives men so crazy?

Tears clouded her eyes as she witnessed Sacha lean in to kiss Ricki. She couldn't watch anymore. She turned and blindly ran out the door, only stopping once outside. Her back against the wall, she sank down, dropping her head in her hands.

"Maddi? Is everything okay?" She looked up to see Jessie crouching beside her.

Jessie.

This affected him too. Maddi sighed, shaking her head.

"I just saw something I wasn't prepared for, even though I probably should've seen it coming." She sniffed, hugging her arms around her legs.

"What happened?"

"I don't think you're going to want to hear this." She frowned, looking up at him.

He let out a sigh. "What's she done now?" His brow furrowed. She could see his jaw tighten, bracing himself for the answer.

"I just walked in on her throwing herself at Ricki. She was all over him, Jessie. I'm pretty sure she kissed him." She looked at him apologetically. If it was hurting her this much when she wasn't even with Ricki, it was bound to be tenfold for Jessie. "Sorry."

"Maddi!" Ricki came running from the studio, Sacha trailing behind, chewing her gum with a grin. "Maddi, it's not what it looks like, nothing happened," he panted.

Jessie stood, chest puffed out. "You kissed Sacha?" he demanded, blocking Ricki's view of Maddi.

"What? No!"

"Oh really? Because Maddi saw it happen." He squeezed his hands into fists at his side. "Are you calling her a liar?"

"No, I mean, I can see how it would look that way…" Jessie's fist connected with his mouth, and he stepped back, hands held up. "Shit, man!" He spat blood from his mouth. "I didn't kiss her, I swear! She tried to kiss me, but I pulled away." He looked at Maddi, his eyes pleading, "I backed away, I swear it. I wouldn't do that to you."

She could see Sacha leaning against the door, a smug look on her face as she inspected her perfectly manicured nails. She was enjoying this. "Even if you didn't kiss her, you still let her think she could. She was all over you." Maddi swallowed the lump in her throat, trying to keep her voice steady. "I get it, okay? You don't want to be with me. I just wish you could've chosen someone else to make your point with." She gathered her things and got up off the ground.

"You want me to walk you home? I don't really feel like being here anymore either," Jessie said, still glaring at Ricki.

"Thanks, but I think I want to be by myself right now." She squeezed his hand before walking away. She turned her head to look at Ricki one last time. There was blood trickling from his nose, and he looked as though he might cry—she wasn't sure if that was from the punch or from being caught out. Either way, she hated seeing him like that. It took every ounce of her strength to keep on walking.

Chapter 13

"He did what?!" Rory gasped. "Well, I definitely didn't see that coming." She quickly covered the ground between her and Maddi and pulled her in for a hug. "What a jackarse!"

"I know, right? I feel so stupid," she mumbled into Rory's shoulder.

"What? Why? You haven't done anything wrong." She pulled her friend out in front of her. "This isn't your fault."

"I know. I just wish I hadn't thrown myself at him the other night. He must think I'm so pathetic."

"Are you kidding? You are a beautiful, fun, loving, warm person, and any guy would be lucky to have you. He's just too stupid to see what he had right in front of him." She paused. "If he can't see how amazing you are, he doesn't deserve you." She brushed the hair off Maddi's face, tucking it behind her ear.

"Have I told you how awesome you are?" Maddi smiled.

"It does sound like something you would say…" Rory joked. "I'm happy to hear it again though, ya know, if you feel you need to." She grinned. Maddi giggled, playfully swatting her arm.

"You are the most awesome person in the history of awesome people. Is that what you wanna hear?"

"Well, if you say so, it must be true." She stood, addressing an imaginary audience, "I'd like to thank my Mum and Dad for making me this awesome. I never could have done it without you guys!" She fanned her face with her hands. "I promised myself I wouldn't cry!" Holding her hands up as if she were examining an award, she continued. "It's nice to be recognised for my awesomeness, and I thank my best friend, Maddi, for bringing that to everyone's attention. I have worked really hard… hey!" She dodged the cushion flying towards her head.

"You're such a clown!"

"An awesome clown though." Rory winked. It was good to see Maddi laughing again. She hated to see her upset and lately it seemed to be that way more often than not. Something would need to be done. It was time to call in the big guns.

As it happened, Damon had had the same thoughts. After Ricki had arrived home with a fat lip and looking sorry for himself, he knew it was time to step in and take action. Someone needed to get these two in line. It was obvious to everyone how crazy they were about each other and how good they were together. Talk about stubborn.

Once Ricki had left for a run the following morning, Damon searched his room for Maddi's address.

It wasn't hard to find. Lucky for him, Ricki had been using it as a bookmark. Pocketing it, he made his way to her place.

When Maddi opened the door, she was surprised to see Damon standing there.

"Hey, gorgeous. You got a minute?"

Maddi couldn't help but smile. "Yeah, of course, Damon. What's up?" she asked, opening the door wider for him to walk through.

"Well, I've got this hankering for a roast, and I was hoping maybe you'd be kind enough to rustle one up?"

Maddi frowned. "What? Right now?"

"No, no, no. That would be rude of me. I mean tonight." He winked.

"I don't know if that's a good idea."

"Aww, go on. No one cooks a feed as good as you," he whined, giving her the ultimate puppy dog eyes. "I've got all the food at home. You don't even have to bring anything."

Laughing, she swiped at his arm. "You do not play fair, Mr. How am I supposed to turn down those eyes?"

Damon beamed. "So that's a yes?"

"It's a *maybe*. Does Ricki know you're here?"

"Nah. I thought I'd surprise him. Let him see what's he's missing, if you know what I mean. You two are made for each other."

"Hey, it's him you need to talk to about that, not me. I told him how I feel, but he turned me down." She plonked herself down on the couch. Damon followed suit. "Did he tell you he kissed Sacha?" She screwed her nose up.

"First up, he didn't kiss her. She was getting all up in his face, and when he realised what she was doing, he pushed her away. He was pretty bummed when he came home last night." He paused, meeting her gaze. "He really turned you down?"

Maddi nodded. "Yup. He said we should just be friends. I mean, I get it. I *am* just out of a relationship and all…"

Damon whistled, shaking his head. "That crazy dumbarse! He never told me *that*." He sat back, looking to the ceiling. "That must've been why he was so quiet the other day. He's a sad sack when you're not around." Sitting up and grabbing her hand, he said, "You gotta come tonight. I know he's been a bit of a dick, but he's so into you. I've never seen him as happy as he is when he's with you."

She smiled sadly. "I thought so too, but what am I supposed to do? I can't make him want me."

"Come tonight. *Show* him. Hell, flirt with me— that ought to do it." He chuckled. "I'll happily make him jealous if it gets him to see sense."

Maddi couldn't help but giggle. She lucked out when she met Ricki, gaining Damon as a friend too. "It might be worth a shot." She thought for a moment before adding, "Okay, I'll come. On one condition. I get to bring Rory with me. She's my flatmate."

"Yeah, of course, whatever you need." He stood, "Yes! Roast for dinner!" Maddi laughed and pushed him towards the door. "Alright, alright, I'm leaving," he said, palms up defensively. He pulled her in for a big bear hug, kissing the top of her head. "We'll sort this out, beautiful." He let go and gave a little wave as he sauntered out the door. "Later!"

"So, what's this Damon like?" Rory asked as they rounded the corner on their way to Ricki's. She had jumped at the chance to tag along and meet the burly guy who was playing match maker. Maddi was glad to have the company; she was anticipating a lot of awkwardness tonight. Even with all that Damon had said, she was still hurting from seeing Ricki with Sacha and didn't really know what to say to him. That was one of the main reasons she wanted Rory with her, to keep her calm. It was her superpower.

"You'll love him. He's like a big teddy bear. And he gives the best hugs."

"Ooh, just the way I like them." She rubbed her hands together before looping her arm through Maddi's. They walked up to the door and knocked.

"Hey, beautiful." Damon grinned at Maddi as he opened the door. "You must be Rory, another looker I see," he said behind his hand to Maddi, making her laugh.

"I like this one." Rory pointed her thumb in Damon's direction as she made her way inside. "Nice place you got here," she added, giving the place the once over.

"You were expecting otherwise?" He clutched at his chest, a mischievous grin on his face.

"Well…" She looked him up and down before grinning. "Nah, just kidding."

Damon chuckled. "I see why she's your best friend. You got a good one here."

"I sure do. We've been besties since pre-school." She smiled at her friend. "I guess I'd better make a start on dinner."

She started rummaging through cupboards, pulling out everything she needed. "You two get acquainted, I've got this." She pushed them out of the kitchen and got to work.

As promised, Damon had provided a chicken to be roasted, along with a selection of veggies. Maddi turned the oven on and began seasoning the bird, humming to herself. She then peeled and chopped potatoes, kumara and yams to add to the pan. She found a can of corn kernels in the cupboard, which she tipped into a saucepan with some water, ready to go on later. The only thing left to organise was the gravy, which she would make while the chicken was resting. Feeling pleased with herself, Maddi turned to join her friends in the other room but came face-to-face with Ricki.

"Oh! I didn't hear you come in. You scared me." She held her hand to her chest, catching her breath. He stood awkwardly in the doorway, rubbing his hand through his hair.

"Sorry, I didn't mean to scare you." He offered a small smile. "I heard the commotion in here and came to investigate. Damon didn't tell me you were coming, but I assume he organised this?"

"Oh, um yeah. I guess it's my turn to apologise then."

"No, I didn't mean… I'm glad you're here." He cleared his throat and shuffled his feet, then shoved his hands in his pockets.

Maddi walked over and wrapped her arms around his shoulders. He sighed and circled his arms around her waist, pulling her in close. "I was worried you wouldn't want to see me anymore." He buried his head in her hair, inhaling her scent.

"You can't get rid of me that easily." She pulled away.

"I hope you know, I never meant to hurt you. You mean too much to me."

"I know. It's forgotten. Come on, let's go see how Rory and Damon are getting on."

Ricki raised his eyebrows. "You left them alone together? That should be interesting." He grinned, rocking back on his heels. He threw an arm around her shoulders as they headed for the living room.

Maddi smiled, leaning into his touch. She hated being mad at him. She hadn't realised how tense she had been until they had embraced. In that instant, all her anger had faded away and she realised something. She wanted Ricki in her life. And if it meant they could only be friends, then that's what she would have to do.

They sat down and enjoyed the meal Maddi had prepared, complete with homemade gravy and all the trimmings. Light banter went back and forth across the table as they each devoured their food and raised their glasses to the chef. Rory and Damon monopolised the conversation, each trying to one up the other with witty comebacks. It was all very entertaining.

Maddi caught Ricki watching her a few times. Not wanting to read anything into it, she just smiled and turned her attention back to Rory, laughing at the jokes she was telling. It made it easier to be around him, having Rory there as a buffer. The light-heartedness of the evening was just what they both needed to get back on track.

Once the table had been cleared, and dishes washed and put away, Rory and Maddi wrapped themselves up in their coats and scarves and said their goodbyes to the boys. They linked arms once again and began their trek home. The air was crisp and they could see their breath, but that didn't dim their moods. Rory kept up an endless chatter—she seemed rather taken by Damon, even if she couldn't see it herself.

Maddi smiled as she listened to her best friend talk. Things were going to be okay. Regardless of what type of relationship she had with Ricki, she just knew that they were meant to be in each other's lives, and she was willing to accept it in any state.

Chapter 14

It was quiet in the studio when Maddi arrived for rehearsals with her girls. She had held try-outs the other night and was pleased with the turn out. This was to be their first rehearsal together, and she was planning on pushing them to their limits. The comps were just around the corner, and she wanted them to be performance ready. Competition would be tough, but she knew what her girls were capable of.

Music filled the room as she went through some stretches and warm-ups. Watching herself in the mirror, she slowly went through the routine she had worked so hard on. If the girls could pull it off—and she had every confidence they would—they had every chance of coming out on top. It hadn't been easy picking the team—she hated to disappoint anyone—but she was happy with her choices. The girls who showed dedication and potential stood out to her, and it was clear to see they had been practicing the steps in class. She needed that kind of effort if they were going to compete against the likes of Sacha.

They all began filing in as she continued to rehearse, each taking out their dance shoes and pulling them on before joining her in the centre of the room. Some did their own warm-ups and others attempted to follow her moves. She smiled, glad to see the initiative they had taken. She had chosen well.

"Alright, girls. We'll do a quick warm-up and then start going through the choreography. I will be working you hard today, so be prepared to sweat. We have a lot to get through before the comps, but I have faith in you." She smiled warmly. "Let's get started, shall we?"

After the warm-up, she broke down the first half of the routine. They went over and over it, perfecting each part before moving onto the next. Once Maddi was satisfied they had it well enough, she put the music on for them to try it at speed.

They had been hard at work for two hours before they stopped for a break, each girl dripping with sweat. Even as tired as they were, there were still plenty of smiles and happy chatter. It pleased Maddi to know they were enjoying it as much as she was.

While they were resting, Maddi described her costume and make up ideas and asked for their opinions as well. They decided on a black leotard with cut-outs around the waist and diamantes of different colours, swirled around the centre and up to the neckline. It would have tassels attached to the lower part to create a skirt, of sorts. Fishnet stockings, and glittery make up would finish the look. As the comps were coming up fast, they would have to do a lot of the work themselves, but they were all eager to help.

They continued to dance for another hour, making the most of their studio time. Maddi had them each take turns at standing down and watching everyone else so they could offer support and suggestions. She had them film what they had done so far, and then did the whole performance to the music for them to watch.

The girls invited her out for a coffee afterwards, which she gratefully accepted.

"Okay, girls, great first practice. Now for the hard part… We need a name!" Maddi declared as she sat down at the table with her hot chocolate.

"Hmmm, how about Sexy Senoritas?" Charlotte suggested.

"Ooh yeah, that sounds good!" Piper agreed. "Or Saucy Salseros?" she added with a giggle.

"Latin Divas."

"Salsa Sweethearts."

"What do you think, Maddi?"

"Hmm, it's a tough one, but I'm leaning more towards Latin Divas."

Piper stood up, holding an imaginary microphone, "Ladies and Gentlemen! Presenting the one and only… Latin Divas!" she bellowed. "Yeah, I like it."

Chuckling, Maddi agreed. "It does have a nice ring to it. Latin Divas it is." She raised her cup in the air. "To the Latin Divas." They clinked their cups together, giggling as droplets of hot chocolate and coffee fell to the table.

Grabbing some napkins, Maddi mopped up the mess. She sat back down and looked around at the girls who would be her shadow for the next month. They were such a charismatic bunch, so full of life—it was easy to get caught up in their energy. Even though this was originally to be a solo piece, she couldn't imagine doing it without these girls now. It felt right to have them be a part of it. They added a completely different feel to it, a different element. As if it was always destined to be this way.

Over the next few weeks, the Latin Divas met every second day for two hours at a time, to go over their competition piece. They all seemed determined to make it flawless, much to Maddi's delight. Not once did they complain about the rigorous schedule, some even still managing to make it to Maddi's shine classes on Tuesdays. To say she was proud was an understatement. These girls had come to mean a great deal to her, providing a much-needed distraction from her feelings towards Ricki. They still spent an awful lot of time together, but it was easier to remain friends alone, now that she was pouring her energy into grooming her Divas for the comps.

There had been many evenings spent blinging their costumes with rhinestones of various colours and patterns. They were beginning to look the part. Even their dance heels had had a spruce up with the shiny stones.

Charlotte had perfected their make-up now too, and that, along with their new and improved costumes, made quite an impression. Maddi had to admit, they looked stunning. She couldn't wait to see how it all looked under the glittering lights of the stage.

The morning of dress rehearsal—full make-up and everything—there was a nervous buzz in the air. They all primped themselves in front of the mirrors, excited to see how it all looked once put together. Charlotte was busy applying black and gold swirls around each of their eyes, dabbing glitter and tiny rhinestones into the paint. Piper was clipping everyone's hair back and spritzing them all with a shimmering hairspray.

Maddi pulled her black fishnets up over her long legs, making sure not to twist them. Her leotard had purple, pink and gold rhinestones in the shape of a star right in the centre, with swirls of each colour around it. She gave herself one final look in the mirror before walking out to the studio to get the music set up. Rory and Ricki were both out their waiting—she had asked them to film it and give some critical feedback.

Rory whistled. "Damn, girl! You look fine!" She drew out the last word, adding a finger snap for emphasis. Maddi chuckled, crossing her leg behind her and lowering into a curtsy.

"Why, thank you." She strutted over to where her iPod was set up, flicking through the playlist until she came to the song she wanted. Turning back to Rory, she pointed at the back of the studio. "I'll get you guys to set up over there, that way the mirror is behind us." Rory nodded, slinging her camera over her shoulder. "Hey, thanks heaps for this, eh?"

"No problemo." Rory saluted before marching to the back of the room. Ricki tagged along, tripod and bags in hand.

Maddi watched them go, her teeth tugging at her bottom lip. She had poured her heart and soul into this choreography and other than her girls, no one else had seen it yet. Even Rory had only been privy to small sections of it. She really hoped they liked it.

The 'Divas' were now in the studio with them, all eager to get moving. During rehearsals, they normally danced in front of the mirrors to ensure their timing was perfect. Maddi had wanted them to do it with the mirrors behind them tonight so they would be prepared for the comps. Bad habits start when you rely on what you see in front of you, and it can be off-putting the first time you face a different direction.

"Alright, girls, you ready? Let's show 'em what we got." She grinned, leading them to their positions. "You ready, Rory?"

"You betcha."

She motioned for Ricki to start the music. The girls, already well-rehearsed, didn't miss a beat; they shimmied and rolled their bodies in perfect unison. Every formation change was flawless, every beat hit with gusto. Maddi had never been prouder.

When they had finished, the air was alive with energy as they bounced about. Gathering around behind Rory, they waited eagerly for her to play back what she had recorded. It looked even better than they had imagined. The costumes and make-up glimmered with every move they made, emphasising the fluidity of their movements.

"I don't care what anyone else says, we rock! We're totally gonna win!" Piper jumped about enthusiastically. She and the others all high-fived one another. Ricki wrapped his hand around Maddi's wrist, pulling her towards him.

"Wow. I don't even know what to say. That was… incredible. You're one hell of a dancer." He looked at her with awe. "And that outfit… you're breath-taking." His eyes raked over her body with appreciation, making her feel both exposed and excited all at once. She knew he only wanted friendship, but his eyes were telling a different story.

"Ah, thanks." Her cheeks warmed, and she glanced at the girls to avoid the way he was making her feel. "I should probably get back to them." She nodded her head in their direction.

"Oh, yeah, of course," he stammered.

Maddi turned and walked awkwardly away, as if she had forgotten how to. Suddenly the Divas seemed as though they were miles away.

Breathe, you idiot.

She could still feel his eyes on her as she finally joined the others. Smiling, she offered her congratulations to them all.

"You guys were great! Absolutely ready for the comps. I'm so proud of you!" She beamed. "One week to go!"

Chapter 15

The next night was another social night out at Feeney's Bar. Maddi and Ricki were going together—as they had been for the last few weeks—and they had managed to convince Damon to come along too; his only condition was that Rory came to keep him company. She was only too happy to oblige.

Ricki and Damon were meeting them at their flat and then they were going to leg it to town. As per usual, the guys arrived on time. Both Rory and Maddi were still applying the finishing touches to their hair and make-up, all the while dancing to a 'Hits of the 80's' CD and singing as loud as possible. Not hearing them enter the room, the girls both squealed when the boys appeared behind them, belting out the words to *Girls Just Wanna Have Fun* and gyrating their hips towards them. They collapsed in fits of laughter.

Once they had composed themselves, Maddi and Rory continued primping themselves, with the boys mimicking them in the background.

"Does this colour suit me?" Ricki asked Damon in a high-pitched voice.

"Oh yeah, totally, it like, makes your lips soooo kissable." He puckered his lips and blew a kiss.

"Oh stop! We're not that bad!" Maddi laughed.

"Nah, I guess not. You know you guys don't need all that crap though, eh?" Damon picked up a handful of cosmetics. "You're stunners just the way you are. Either of you could have any guy you want." Maddi looked at him in the mirror with an eyebrow raised. *If only*, she thought. He shrugged, looking sheepish as he realised what he'd said. "Sorry" he mouthed.

"Any guy, huh?" Rory asked. "That sounds like a challenge." Damon chuckled, throwing his arm around her shoulders.

"Hey now, no need to go crazy. They have to get through me first." He gave her arm a wee squeeze before tickling her ribs. Rory pretended to struggle against him, but the contentment in her eyes and the flush of her cheeks made it obvious how she felt. Maddi would put money on the two of them ending up together.

Feeney's Bar was just starting to get busy when they arrived. Rory and Maddi grabbed their usual table by the dancefloor, while the boys went to the bar to order their drinks. There were a number of people milling about but no one actually dancing yet. Rory liked to watch people and wager who would brave the floor first. Feeling bold, Maddi strutted up to Ricki and slipped her hand in his. Nodding to the dancefloor, she raised her brow in question.

"Shall we dance?"

"Yeah, sure." He allowed himself to be led to the empty space. It was one of their favourite songs playing, so he could hardly turn her down. He was getting used to dancing in front of others now, in fact, he didn't even notice them anymore. He had eyes only for Maddi.

Even amongst all her troupe training, they had still managed to find time to practice together, and they always made it to Feeney's for a night out. They were living and breathing salsa and loving every minute of it.

After dancing for four songs straight, they headed back to the table for a breather and a drink. Rory and Damon were deep in conversation.

"Seriously? Any superpower in the world, and you would choose speed?"

"Yeah, you know, like *The Flash*. That'd be awesome!"

"No, I'd much rather be able to fly."

"Boring! Come on, Rory, think about it, I could get the shit jobs done super-fast, and then have more time to do what I wanna do. Hell, I could run to Dunedin and back, just to get you a coffee!" Rory rolled her eyes, but she couldn't help but laugh.

"Okay, that would be pretty sweet," she conceded as she turned towards Maddi and Ricki. "Hey, guys, having fun?"

"Clearly not as much as you two," Maddi said with a smirk on her face. "You gonna get up and have a dance too? You should drag this one with you." She poked Damon in the arm as she took a seat. "You could show him a thing or two."

"You know, I just might." Rory stood and, latching onto Damon's hand, she pulled him out of his seat. "Come on, let's see what you can do, Speedy." Maddi could hear her giggling as they made their way out to the middle of the packed dancefloor. She swivelled back to face Ricki, her eyes alight with glee at the thought of those two together. Ricki laughed.

"I know that look. What are you planning?" He leaned in conspiratorially. As he bent his head towards her, she caught a glimpse of the door and sucked in a breath. Dane had just entered the bar with a group of dancers. She shouldn't have been surprised; they had both frequented the place before everything went to custard, she just hadn't seen him in weeks. True to his word, he had in fact left her alone—not even coming to their classes. Maddi had welcomed the break from him. The classes with Ricki as her partner ran smoothly, and her dance troupe was gaining momentum. Things had been great without his overbearing presence in her life.

As her smile waivered, Ricki followed her gaze. He too had relished the respite from all the aggression Dane had caused. He had quite enjoyed hanging out with Maddi free of stress and interruptions. It was selfish of him, he knew, but he had been hoping Dane wouldn't return.

Reaching across the table, he held her hand, rubbing circles around her wrist with his thumb.

"You okay? We can leave if you want." He looked at her with such concern, she thought she might burst into tears if she didn't look away.

"No, it's okay. I'm not going to let him ruin our night." She forced a smile on her face. "You want to dance again?"

"Of course." He smiled warmly, trying to ease the tension emanating off her. They made their way to the middle of the crowded floor, hiding among their peers. Ricki pulled her in close and, with his thumb and finger, he tilted her chin upwards.

"Forget about him. We're here to have fun, remember?" He kissed her forehead before spinning her out to his side. Maddi squealed, grinning. It worked every time. Spinning her back into him, he took her through several long combos, keeping her on her toes. She was puffing and bright-eyed by the end of the song.

"Thanks for that. I needed it." She smiled, walking back to their table once more. Rory and Damon were at the bar getting more drinks. The bartender placed a round of shots on a tray and handed it to Rory.

"I, ah, thought you could use one of these." Rory gestured to the drinks as she placed the tray on the table. "Bottoms up!" They all downed their Sambuca's in one go, slamming the glasses on the table after.

"Aagghh! I forgot how much I hate that stuff!" Maddi waved her hands in the air and jumped up and down. She shook her head, reaching for another. "Salute!" They lifted their glasses in the air before shooting them back.

"Woo! I feel good!" Rory stuck her black tinged tongue out. "We should dance some more!" She grabbed Maddi's hand and proceeded to bump and grind right there on the spot. The boys were only too happy to watch, even yelling out encouragement.

"Yeow! Shake it, baby!" Damon whistled, clapping his hands together, enjoying every second of the show. Maddi and Rory exchanged a knowing look. Grinning, they both pounced on him until he had no choice but to join in.

"If I'm dancing, so are you!" He gripped Ricki's arm and dragged him up too. They continued dancing in their own little circle, trying to out-do each other. It wasn't long before they were collapsing on their chairs, cheeks sore from laughing so much.

"That… was… so… fun!" Rory panted, clutching her knees as she tried to catch her breath. Maddi was rubbing her face.

"I haven't laughed so much in ages!"

"Me neither!" Damon added, gulping back the rest of his vodka. "You guys want another?" He shook his glass in the air. There was a chorus of yes, so he stumbled to the bar.

"I'll go help him," Rory offered.

"You wanna get some air?" Ricki yelled over the music.

"Sure, that'd be good." Maddi stood, seizing his hand. The burst of fresh air on their faces felt amazing, instantly cooling them down. Maddi dropped her head back, closing her eyes as she let the wind blow over her.

There was a little cough from beside the entrance. Dane stepped out from the shadows.

"Ah, hi." He waved. "How've you been? You look good." His eyes raked over her body and back to her face. "Real good."

Maddi's skin crawled. It was as though he was undressing her with his eyes. He had a hint of a smile on his lips, enjoying her discomfort. "I was hoping I might run into you tonight. Thought maybe we could have a drink, ya know, for old times' sake."

Maddi didn't want to do *anything* with him, let alone have a drink, but what could she do? It would be rude to turn him down.

"Um, yeah, sure," she mumbled. Still holding Ricki's hand, she could feel his body tense up against her. She gave his hand a gentle squeeze, looking up at him over her shoulder. "One drink." She mouthed before turning her attention back to Dane. He rested his hand on her lower back to guide her through the doors and to a table away from the busy crowd. Glancing around, she saw Rory with a look of loathing on her face, her hands balled into fists. She marched towards them, but Maddi shook her head. She needed to do this.

Chapter 16

He pulled a chair out for her. She perched on the edge of it, her hands in her lap.

"Still drinking vodka and Red Bull?" he asked, pulling his wallet out of his pocket.

"Um, yeah thanks." She smiled weakly. Fidgeting in her seat, she kept looking back to her friends. Rory was glaring at the back of Dane's head as he ordered drinks at the bar. Ricki was pacing beside the table, glancing up at her every few steps. Damon looked as though he was trying to calm him down. As nervous as she was to be here, she was relieved to know that her friends all had her back if anything went down.

Dane, ignoring Rory's stare, carried their drinks back to the table. Ordinarily he would have stopped and chatted to others, but tonight he had his eyes fixed on Maddi. It unnerved her. She had to keep breaking eye contact; it was just too intense and confrontational. There was something about the *way* he watched her that put her on edge.

Handing Maddi her drink, he took his place opposite her, pulling his chair in close. He reached for her hand across the table. Slowly stroking her thumb with his.

"I'm so glad you're here, Maddi. You look amazing, as always."

Shifting uncomfortably, she glanced up at him. "Thanks," she said. She shifted her hand, but he held firm.

"I never told you enough how beautiful you were… *are*. You should be told every day how brilliant you are." He continued stroking her hand and staring into her eyes. Unsure what to say, Maddi gave a little shrug and smiled. "Never were good at taking compliments, were you?" He chuckled.

"Your compliments usually required an expectation on my part," she said calmly, lifting her eyes to meet his once more. He pulled his hand away, leaning back on his chair.

"Ouch." He held his hand to his heart. "I deserved that, though. You're right. I've done a lot of thinking these past few weeks, and I realise what a dick I was being."

"I'm listening." She folded her arms across her chest.

He grinned. "You're gorgeous when you're being stubborn, ya know?"

"Quit it with the compliments, it's weird. You said you wanted to talk about something?"

His brow furrowed. "I wasn't a complete jerk, was I? I mean, you *were* happy with me at one point, weren't you?" His eyes pleaded.

Sighing, Maddi replied, "There were good times, in the beginning at least. I was just so tired of being compared to *her* all the time and treated like my opinions didn't matter."

"Who?"

"What?"

"You said you were tired of being compared to *her*. Who was I comparing you to?"

She rolled her eyes. "Oh, come on, Dane. Like you don't know." He stared blankly. "Um, your ex, Sacha. Ring any bells?"

He sucked air in through his teeth. "You thought I was comparing you two? Maddi, she cheated on me and stole my work. Why would I compare you to *her*?"

"You didn't trust me because of her. You didn't let me have any say in our dancing because of her. She was the third party in our relationship, and I let it go on too long. Constantly hearing about your boyfriend's ex and how good a dancer she is eventually takes its toll."

Dane rubbed his hands over his face and through his hair to rest on the back of his neck.

"I don't know what to say. I guess I just never thought about it that way. I was so scared of losing you that I got a bit too controlling, I guess. I'm so sorry, Maddi. I never meant to make you feel that way."

"I know you didn't."

"I'd like to make it up to you." He rested his elbows on the table, tapping his fingers to the beat.

"That's not necessary. Let's just put it in the past."

"I think it is necessary. We'll never get past it if I don't make amends."

"Wait, what?"

"Well, we can't move forward in our relationship if you still hold it against me, can we? So, I have to do something to make it better." He continued drumming his fingers on the table, watching them as he did so.

"What relationship, Dane?" She swallowed, the hair on the back of her neck standing as she waited for his response.

"What do you mean? You and me." He motioned between them. "I did what you asked and gave you space to think, and I did the same. I think we can still make it work. We can go back to where we left off." He smiled and reached for her hand again.

She pulled away, flicking her eyes to her friends' table to check they were still there. She could see all eyes watching their every move. "Ah, I think you are a bit confused. We can't go back to where we left off."

"No." He shook his head. "You're right, we want to move forward not backwards."

"No, that's not what I mean." She looked him in the eye to make sure he really heard her this time. "I don't want to go back at all."

"I gave you nearly a month to think about things, and I'm willing to work on stuff, so what's the problem?"

"Dane, I don't want to be with you. That's kind of a big problem, wouldn't you say? This space that I've had has been a welcome change. For the first time in ages, I feel like *me* again. I've got other things going on in my life now. And… I'm happy." She whispered the last part, afraid of hurting him.

"No. That's not right. You said you just needed space and time to think. You didn't say we were over for good." He frowned.

"I told you I didn't want to see you anymore. Remember?"

"Yeah, but I… I went away. I gave you what you needed." He was speaking slowly and clearly, making sure she heard what he was saying.

"I think maybe you got the wrong idea. I'm sorry, Dane. I don't think we're good together. Please accept it." She stood on shaking legs. "I have to go."

"That looked intense," Rory said as Maddi sat down.

"You could say that." She glanced over at Dane, who was still staring after her with a confused look on his face. "He seems really mixed up. I don't know if he's talked himself into thinking we're still together or what."

"He thinks you're still together? Oh, that's fucked up."

"Hmmm," Maddi agreed. She was worried about him. Something didn't seem quite right about him. It was as though something had snapped. She hoped he would be alright.

"You okay?" Ricki asked as he joined them at the table.

"Yeah, I'm fine." She smiled. "I could really do with another drink though."

"On it!" Damon called on his way to the bar.

"That bad, huh? How about a dance to make you feel better?" Ricki offered his hand, which she accepted.

"You read my mind." She allowed herself to be led to the dancefloor, wanting to forget what had happened.

Dane looked on with a sadness in his eyes. He stood up and strode out the door.

Chapter 17

After an hour of letting loose on the dancefloor, Maddi and Ricki sauntered towards their table, ready for a much-needed break. They dripped with sweat and panted as they tried to catch their breath. The discussion with Dane was a distant memory now.

Their table was empty, save for a few scattered shot glasses from earlier. Maddi noted that Rory's bag was missing, and so was Damon's jacket.

"I think we've been ditched," she stated with a grin, waving her hands at the empty spaces.

"I think you might be right. Do you think they hooked up?" Ricki asked, returning the grin.

"I'd bet money on it." Maddi laughed. "About bloody time too!" She threw herself into one of the chairs. "I'm knackered."

"Yeah, me too. You want another drink, or you want to go home?" he asked, reaching for his wallet.

"Maybe one more before we hit the road."

"Okay, be right back," he said as he walked up to the bar once more. Maddi watched him go, thinking about how much she enjoyed being with him. His friendship meant the world to her. She knew she was probably setting herself up for heartbreak, but there was something intoxicating about him—she couldn't give him up. As if he could feel her watching, he turned and smiled back at her, that lop-sided, sexy grin she loved so much. She grinned back, wiggling her fingers in a small wave.

He casually strolled over with their drinks in hand, never taking his eyes off her. Surely he felt the chemistry between them? The way he looked at her—as though there was no one else in the room—undid her. Her heart fluttered in her chest the closer he got. She would give anything to feel his lips on hers, even just briefly. Trying to calm her heart and head, she rummaged through her bag, looking for something to distract herself with. There was no telling how much longer she could sit idly by and not throw herself into his arms.

"Here you go, Maddi." He handed her a drink, which she happily accepted, taking a large gulp.

"Thanks, I needed that." She bent down to untie the straps on her dance shoes. She put them into their bag and reached for her street shoes. She wiggled her toes. Street shoes always felt so foreign after she'd been dancing. Dance heels mould to the shape of your feet, so the fit was as close to perfect as you could get. She could dance for hours on end with them on and not bat an eye. Sitting up again, she took another mouthful of the cool liquid.

"You okay?" Ricki asked.

"Yeah, I'm fine. Just tired I guess."

"You want to head off?" Ricki stood, gulping down the last of his drink and offering her his hand.

"Um sure, if that's okay." She quickly sculled back the rest of her vodka and grabbed hold of his hand. She found herself admiring those strong hands of his. They were much bigger than hers, the perfect size for hers to fit into. The rough calluses on his palm were a contrast to the softness of the rest of his hand. She couldn't help but wonder what they would feel like on her body.

"Shall we go?" he prompted. Maddi nodded, snatching up her bag and shoes before following him to the door.

They walked hand-in-hand—as they did so often now— all the way home. Anyone could be mistaken for assuming they were, in fact, a couple. The way they interacted with each other screamed intimacy.

Maddi giggled as they discussed their missing friends and their whereabouts.

"Do you think they're at your place or mine?"

"Who says they even made it that far?" Ricki joked. Maddi swatted his arm.

"Ewwww! Mental pictures!" Ricki chuckled at the face she was making. "God, I hope they're actually in a bedroom and we don't walk in on them." She shook her body in disgust. Ricki tipped his head back, laughing even harder. Maddi frowned at him, the corners of her mouth lifting slightly as she fought off the bubbling laughter inside, until she could no longer contain it. She clutched her stomach as she laughed, tears forming in the corners or her eyes. Every time she stopped, she'd look at Ricki, and they'd both burst into yet another fit of laughter.

"Oh God. I haven't laughed that much since… since I don't even know when." Maddi swiped the tears away as she began to laugh again.

Ricki smiled, nudging her with his elbow. "Shall we carry on? I'm sure they'll be done by now." He winked.

"They better be." She grinned up at him. She ever so elegantly, straightened, reaching for his arm to steady herself as the ground swam before her eyes. "I may have had a little more to drink than I thought." She giggled.

"Come on, you." Ricki swung his arm around her shoulder to hold her up as they continued their trek home. Taking advantage of the opportunity, Maddi snuggled in closer.

"Mmm, you're warm." She wrapped one arm around his back and the other around his waist to meet. His grip tightened, securing her in his embrace.

"Let's get you home to the fire." He quickened his pace. They continued walking in silence, the cold making their breath visible. Ricki slowly rubbed his hand up and down Maddi's arm, keeping her warm. A part of her wanted to slow down, so that she would have an excuse to cuddle into him for longer. It was so nice and comforting being in his arms. He wasn't a big guy, but she felt safe when she was with him. Something she had never felt with Dane.

"Almost there. I'll come in and stoke the fire for you, if you like," he offered. Maddi smiled; she had lived there with Rory for a while now and they had managed fine by themselves, but the sentiment was nice anyway.

"Sure, that would be great. I could even rustle us up a hot chocolate while you do that."

"Sounds great. That should be enough to keep me warm before I head back to mine." He smiled down at her. Tempted as she was to offer for him to stay over—on the couch of course—she thought better of it. Things had been ticking along nicely between them and she was scared to put herself out there again. Instead, she just returned his smile.

The house was dark with no signs of life. Maddi rummaged through her bag for the keys.

"Looks like they made it to your place after all." She grinned at him.

"Looks like it." He followed her in, closing the door behind them. "Lucky me," he deadpanned. They walked into the lounge where the fire still had a faint glow. "I'll get this baby pumping. Can't have you catching a cold so close to the comps now, can we?" He got to work bringing in some large logs of wood and stacked them beside the fire for her. She switched the jug on and grabbed two cups down off the shelf, scooping some cocoa into each one. Hunting through the cupboards, she triumphantly brought out a bag of marshmallows that had been hiding in the back.

"Look what I found." She waved them in the air before dropping several on top of their steaming mugs. She joined him on the couch in front of the fire, the flames flickering light on their faces. She handed him his mug.

"I had a really good night tonight."

"Yeah, me too."

He pulled his lips to the side, peeking sideways at her. "So… Do you want to talk about the whole Dane thing? It looked kind of intense."

"Um, yeah, it was." She frowned. "He was acting as though we were still a couple. Like he was just giving me space and then we'd be good as new."

Ricki whistled low. "Wow. That *is* weird." His brows furrowed. "You think he got the message and he'll leave you alone now?"

"I don't know. I hope so." She paused, staring into her drink. "I do feel sorry for him though. He seemed so confused. It's like his brain won't let him process that we broke up." She blew on her hot chocolate before taking a sip.

"Hmm. I don't like it. You need to keep your doors locked, just in case. I don't really like the idea of you being alone." He looked into her eyes, concern all over his face. It was the perfect opportunity to ask him to stay, but again, she couldn't bring herself to do it.

"I'm sure it'll be fine. He didn't hang around at the pub after our talk so maybe it has sunk in now." She nodded as if agreeing with herself. "Anyway, it's late, I'm sure he went home already. And Rory is generally here with me. I'll be fine." She stared into the fire, deep in thought.

"If you're sure?" He placed his hand on her knee, once again looking into her eyes. "You can text me or call anytime, okay? Even if you just get scared." He squeezed her knee. "Promise me you'll call me if you need me."

"I promise." She smiled, placing her hand over his.

Taking advantage of the dark night, Dane huddled down in a bush outside Maddi's place. He had wandered aimlessly through the streets after they had had their talk and eventually found himself at her house. The lights were off, so he knew she wasn't home yet.

He couldn't shake the feeling that something was going on between her and Ricki. They looked far too cosy at Feeney's. Determined to get to the bottom of it, he stalked around the outside of her home, looking for any signs of his presence. He tried each of the doors and windows to see if he could get in, but they were all shut tight. In the end he had settled for hiding in the bushes, waiting for her to come home.

When he saw them arrive, all cosy in each other's arms, his blood had boiled. He positioned himself behind a bush outside the lounge window. He needed to see for himself if there was anything there. He needed to see what he was up against. She had said she didn't want to be with him anymore, but he wasn't going to accept that. He needed her. She *belonged* to him.

From his vantage point, he could see them happily playing house; getting the fire cranking and having hot drinks on the couch—the couch where he and Maddi had shared many drinks together—how cosy. It all looked innocent, until he saw Ricki put his hand on her.

And the look in her eyes was one that he was all too familiar with. He should know; it was the way she used to look at him, back when they first got together. It was a slap in the face. The sudden stabbing pain in his heart made him catch his breath. He clutched at his chest, unable to turn away from what he was witnessing. They sat that way, holding hands, for quite some time before Ricki finally stood up to leave. He watched as Maddi walked him to the door and saw them embrace before saying goodbye.

Dane waited until he was sure Ricki would be far enough away, then he slowly, silently stepped out of the shadows and walked calmly to the door.

Chapter 18

Ricki unlocked the door to his place, jingling the keys loudly to prepare anyone in the house of his arrival. The lights were on, and empty wine glasses sat on the table, with an open bottle of wine between them. Rory's jacket was draped across one of the chairs, and her heels had been discarded by the couch.

He threw his jacket on the coat hook and switched the jug on to make a coffee. Taking a cup down from the shelf he then searched the drawer for a clean spoon. After coming up empty, he rinsed one that had been sitting in the sink. Scraping the last of the coffee into his cup, he scrawled himself a note on the whiteboard to buy both coffee and spoons.

The sound of giggling came from Damon's room as he walked past. Ricki had a little chuckle to himself as he retrieved his phone from his pocket to ring Maddi and let her know they were there and check that she was okay on her own.

He walked into his room, shutting the door behind him as he punched in her number. She didn't answer. She must've gone straight to bed after he left. He sent her a message, filling her in so she wouldn't be worried. He sat on his bed, sipping his drink and kicking his shoes off. The walk home had woken him up, so he grabbed his book from his nightstand, turning to the marked page.

He settled back against his pillow, but before he could get too comfortable, his phone began to vibrate. Maddi's picture flashed up on the screen. Grinning, he answered.

"Hey, did you get my text? … Maddi?" The sound was muffled as if in a pocket. She must have butt dialled. "Maddi?" he said louder, hoping she would hear his voice and pick up.

"…Dane, please don't. You're scaring me…"

"Maddi?" he asked again, sitting up. His heart thundered in his chest.

"…Don't touch me!"

"Oh shit!" He quickly hung up the phone and grabbed his shoes, banging on the wall to alert Damon.

I never should have left her.

He thumped the wall again.

"Kinda busy, man!" came Damon's response.

"Sorry, but this is an emergency!" he yelled. "Maddi's in trouble. We need to get over there now!" He heard them scurrying around as they threw clothes on and ran out to join him.

"What's going on?" Rory demanded, pulling her heels on once more.

"I don't know. I just got a call from Maddi, and all I could hear was her pleading with Dane, she sounded really scared. We've got to go!"

"Oh my God! Maddi!" Rory's face went pale.

After Ricki had left, Maddi had started getting herself organised for bed. She had just changed into her nightie and was heading for the bathroom when she heard a knock at the door. Smiling to herself, she quickly ran to open it, her robe flowing open behind her.

"Okay what did you forget?" she asked before realising it was Dane at the door and not Ricki. "Oh, hi," she said. A wave of unease washed over her. She clutched her robe around her, shifting from one foot to the other.

"Hey, Maddi." Dane raked his hand through his hair. "I was in the neighbourhood…" He drifted off, his eyes wandering until they rested on the small spot of bare skin he could see at the top of her robe. "I really had to see you. I didn't like where we left things at Feeney's, you know?" He stepped towards her, looking into her eyes.

Backing away, Maddi said, "Dane, it's late. Can this wait? I really just want to get to bed." She reached for the door, but his hand flew out and stopped her.

"It won't take long, Maddi." He took another step forward, blocking the doorway with his foot.

"I… ah…"

"I need you, Maddi. I always have. You need me too." He was staring down at her, slowly easing his way further into the house.

"I'd like you to leave please," she said, raising her chin in defiance.

"I'm not ready to leave yet. We have things to sort out." He looked back to where her robe was loose, a hint of a smile playing on his lips.

"Dane, please don't. You're scaring me. I'd like you to leave."

"I would never hurt you, you know that, Maddi. I just want to love you." He reached a finger out to stroke down the side of her face. Maddi froze in fear. He continued to drag his finger down her neck, towards the top of her robe.

"Don't touch me!" she screamed, swatting his hand away. His face twisted in pain.

"I need to show you, Maddi. Would you just stop fighting me and let me show you?" He was breathing down on her, one hand grasping her wrist, while the other pushed the door closed behind him. "I just want to love you," he whispered again, cupping his hand behind her neck, leaning in as if to kiss her. He grinned as he began dragging her towards her bedroom.

"Dane, please. Don't." She fought against him, trying frantically to get out of his grip, but he was much stronger than she was. He kicked the door to her room open and led her inside. Tears were streaming down her face as she continued to beg. "You don't have to do this."

"Yes. I do. You need to see. I have to show you. We were made for each other." He pressed on her shoulders, making her sit on the edge of the bed. He grabbed the collar of her robe and slipped it off her shoulders, revealing her silky nightie. "God, you're so beautiful," he whispered, leaning down to nuzzle into her neck. Maddi closed her eyes.

"I love you so much, Maddi. You'll see." He kissed her neck and up towards her mouth. She turned her head away. Sighing, he stood and pulled his shirt off over his head. Maddi scrambled up the bed, away from him. "Now, now." He crawled up to follow. "Don't be a little cock tease." He slammed his fists against the mattress. Panting, he grabbed her ankles and yanked hard, bringing her back to the edge of the bed and underneath him. "Stop fighting me, goddamn it!" He pinned her wrists above her head with one hand, while the other was busily undoing the zipper on his pants. Maddi squirmed beneath him, but his grip was too tight. She was trapped.

This is it. This is actually happening right now.

"Dane, please, don't do this," she begged once more, looking into his eyes, hoping to see a glimmer of empathy.

"I'm not going to hurt you. I promise." He smiled, lowering his body onto hers, making it impossible for her to move. She turned her head to look out the window, trying to shut her brain off so that she didn't have to be present while this was going on. Her silent tears were pooling on the bed sheet as she gave up fighting.

"Look at me, Maddi," he whispered into her ear, but she couldn't hear him anymore. "I said, look at me!" He clutched her face in one hand and pulled her to look at him. Her eyes had glazed over. She was no longer present. There were voices in her head, calling her name. They kept repeating it over again.

"Maddi!" It was Rory. It sounded so real, like she was in the room with her.

"Get off her!" Dane was lifted and thrown up against the wall. She could see Ricki holding Dane by the neck, he reared his hand back and punched him in the face, again and again until Damon grabbed his arm and pulled him away.

"Ricki, stop! He's had enough."

"Oh God!" she cried, her hands covering her mouth as she shook her head. Rory rushed in and jumped on the bed, wrapping Maddi in her arms, rocking her back and forth.

"Shhhh, hon. It's over. You're okay," she kept repeating through tears of her own. "You're okay." Maddi gripped onto her friend, scared to let go. She stared at the limp body of the man who had only moments before been tormenting her. His face was slick with blood from his nose. It looked broken.

"Is… is he dead?" she whispered.

"No. He should be, but no," Damon said, finally releasing his friend. "Let the cops sort him out now, Ricki."

"Yeah, yeah." Turning to Maddi, he asked, "Are you okay?" Those three little words were enough to let loose another onslaught of tears. Her face crumpled, and her body sagged with the weight of what had just happened. Ricki ran to her, enveloping her in his arms, holding her up.

"I'm here now. I won't let anything happen to you. You're safe." He kissed the top of her head, resting his cheek against her. "You're safe now."

"I'll call the cops before he wakes up. Damon, keep an eye on him," Rory said as she ran from the room.

"Of course." Damon stood over Dane's body, watching for any signs of movement.

"How did you know?" Maddi sniffed.

"What?"

"How did you know he was here? That I needed you?" She lifted her head to look up at him.

"Your phone. You rang me. I could hear you… him…"

"But I didn't…" She looked at her discarded robe. "I must've knocked it. It was in my pocket."

"Good thing you had it on you."

Rory walked back into the room. "They're on their way." She sat next to Maddi. "I'm so sorry."

"What for?"

"If I hadn't disappeared on you, you wouldn't have been here alone." Rory looked down at her hands as she twisted them together on her lap. "I'm so selfish."

"You couldn't have known this would happen. You're allowed to have a life," Maddi said, slipping her hand into her friend's. "I knew something wasn't right with him. I just never thought he'd do… something like this. I just can't believe it." Her eyes glistened with fresh tears at the thought of what very nearly happened.

"You're safe now. I won't let him near you again," Ricki said tightening his grip.

Dane came to but was kept under the watchful eye of Damon. Ricki had led Maddi out of the room and to the warmth of the lounge, while Rory made her a hot drink. Damon held Dane hostage until the police arrived quarter of an hour later.

Maddi had given her statement, and Dane had been taken away. He had attempted to apologise to her as he was being escorted to the awaiting vehicle, but she had turned her back on him. He had had enough chances as far as she was concerned.

Damon joined Rory in her room, and Ricki curled up beside Maddi on the floor in the lounge. She couldn't face her room. Ricki held her in his arms all night. She clung to him, calling out in her sleep as she re-lived her nightmare, and every time, he would whisper that she was safe, stroking her face to calm her. It pained him to know that this could have been avoided if he had just insisted on staying with her like he'd wanted to.

Chapter 19

The day of the comps was looming, and Maddi was only just recovering from her ordeal with Dane. She was fine during the day, but the evenings were when she found it hard. The sight of her bedroom would send her into a panic attack, so she barely went in there anymore. Rory decided that a change was in need, and after recruiting the boys to help, they moved all her furniture out and into the spare room. She bought new bed sheets and duvets and rid her drawers of any reminders of Dane. When they were finished, she felt much better.

The boys stayed again. Maddi didn't seem to be able to sleep without the extra company. As a thank you to her friends for all their help, she shouted fish 'n' chips and beer for tea. Rory and Damon had gone out to pick it up and stop at the DVD store on the way back. They were planning on just a quiet, relaxing night at home, before the pressure of the comps the next day.

Maddi was a little nervous about how she would go with her performance—she wasn't exactly feeling sexy. Far from it in fact. The thought of prancing around in front of all those people, in an outfit that leaves little to the imagination, was more than a little daunting. She wasn't sure she could do it, but her girls were counting on her. They had worked so hard to get here, she couldn't let them down now. The Divas didn't know what had happened, and unless she wanted to divulge that information, she had no choice but to go on.

After the movie, Damon and Rory retired to her room for the night—they had become virtually inseparable these days. Maddi was so happy for them; she had never seen her friend like this before.

It must be love, she thought with a smile.

Ricki and Maddi headed for her room. They climbed into bed and assumed their usual position—Ricki on his back, with Maddi tucked in under his arm, her head resting on his chest. Just having him near her was enough to make her feel safer. Even though Dane had been arrested, she couldn't shake the fear that he would return, and Ricki seemed more than happy to keep her company each night. He gently stroked her arm.

"Are you ready for tomorrow?" he asked.

"Mmm, I guess so. I'm a bit... I don't know..." She paused, trying to think of the words to say. "It feels weird to be dancing in those clothes, and in that way. You know, after..." She trailed off.

"What do you mean? You're a fantastic dancer and you look great in that outfit."

"I feel very exposed in it. You don't think it's a bit... provocative?" She looked up at him.

"Maddi, you don't think what happened was your fault, do you? Because I can tell you right now, it wasn't. You did nothing wrong. You can't shut yourself away and hide. He wins then." He lifted her chin. "You are gorgeous, and the best dancer I know. You and your girls have put so much into this. You deserve to show everyone your routine and how hard you've worked. Don't let him take that away from you."

She smiled a sad smile. "It's just. I'm scared. What if he gets out? What if he shows up?" Her eyes welled up, tears spilling over her lashes and onto his chest. Ricki sat up, pulling her with him.

"That's not going to happen. I won't let him come near you again. Okay?"

"Okay." She sniffed, nodding. "Thank you."

"Hey, I told you, any time you need me, I'll be there, and I meant it. You're stuck with me." He smiled down at her.

She smiled back. "You're so good to me."

The next morning, Ricki snuck out of bed early and prepared a massive feast of scrambled eggs, sausages, and hash browns for everyone. He had a pot of coffee brewing and had even set the table up with placemats and cutlery. The whole shebang. When Maddi walked out to see what he was up to, she was pleasantly surprised.

"What's all this?"

"It's the day of the comps. I thought you could use a decent feed to help get you through the day." He grinned at her. "Coffee?" he asked, holding the pot in the air.

"Mmm, please," she said, taking a seat at the table.

"Is that coffee I smell?" Damon stumbled out to the lounge wearing only a pair of boxers.

"Yeah, it is. Get it while it's hot," Ricki said, "And put some clothes on, man." He laughed. Damon gave him the finger as he made his way to the bathroom.

"Here you go, beautiful." Ricki placed a plate down in front of Maddi and one for himself. "I hope you're hungry." He ran back to the kitchen to retrieve the coffee and milk. "Can't forget that now."

"Something smells A-Maze-Ing!" Rory called as she bounced out of her room and into the lounge. "Did you do this?" she asked Ricki as she swiped a piece of toast from the table, taking a bite.

"Sure did. Help yourself, there's plenty."

"Mmm, don't mind if I do." She helped herself to a plate and proceeded to load it up. Ricki whistled.

"Damn, girl, you can eat. You are perfect for Damo." He laughed. Rory just smiled and threw her crust at him.

"Hey, a girl's gotta build up her strength for all the bedroom gymnastics going on in there." Ricki almost choked on his coffee.

"Too much information." He laughed. Damon came out of the bathroom, scratching his head.

"Babe, have you seen my shirt?" He searched around the lounge. "Never mind." He dragged a tee out from under the couch, pulling it over his head before joining them at the table.

"Rory's just telling us about the bedroom gymnastics." Maddi grinned.

"Oh yeah? You should see it. Damn, my girl can bend." He winked and blew a kiss in Rory's direction.

"Thanks, babe," she said, catching his kiss and holding it to her heart. She jumped up and sat on his lap, dragging her plate with her. Damon circled an arm around her waist and then reached over to steal one of her hash browns. She promptly smacked the back of his hand with her fork. "Hey, I need that. This," she motioned to her body, "doesn't bend without sustenance."

Chuckling, Damon grabbed his own plate and started piling food on it. "Fair call," he said.

"So, Maddi, I had an idea I wanted to run by you," said Ricki.

"Yeah, what's that?"

"Well, I thought that maybe we could dance together. Tonight." He looked at her, a twinkle in his eye.

"At the after party? I wasn't planning on going to that."

"Okay, firstly we need to address that. Why wouldn't you go?"

"You know why."

"When you guys win—and you will—your girls are going to want to celebrate. With you, their leader. You have to go. Even if it's just for an hour. And of course you'll dance with me there." Maddi put her fork down and clasped her hands over her plate.

"I guess…"

Ricki rested his hand on hers. "I know." He looked at Rory for support.

"You guys are totally gonna nail it tonight, hon. We'll be there to watch and cheer you on too, won't we, Damo?"

"Wouldn't miss it."

"What I actually meant though, is that maybe we could enter together?" Ricki stared into her eyes, waiting for her reaction.

"We have nothing prepared though," she said.

"That's not entirely true. We've been working really hard, and I know we can do it. You and Dane were registered to compete already, so…" He winced, bracing himself for her reaction. "I changed the names on the form," he said hesitantly.

"You entered us already?"

"Ah, yeah." He looked down at his plate, suddenly not hungry anymore. This was not the reaction he'd been hoping for. "I thought it would be a nice surprise for you. I asked Lisa if we could change the names, a few weeks ago."

"I… I don't know."

"Maddi." He pulled his chair closer to hers and clasped both her hands in his. "We can do this. Do you trust me?"

"Yes." She nodded, biting her lip to stop the quivering.

"Hey." He lifted her chin. "We can do this," he said again.

"You guys will be great!" Rory added. "We can go shopping and find you a new dress to wear if you want. We still have a few hours before you need to head down there." Maddi smiled at her friend. "Oh, this is so exciting! Shopping!"

"Thanks, Rory. That would be great." She squeezed Ricki's hand.

"So, that's a yes?"

She nodded. "I mean, I guess." She bit her lip, nodding. "Yes. It's a yes."

Down at the auditorium there was a hive of activity. Groups were rehearsing on the stage to get their positioning, while others were backstage putting their make up on and slicking their hair back. Rory had tagged along to help with the preparations before she had to head back to her seat with Damon. With her help, Maddi had found the perfect dress for her performance with Ricki. It was a fitted, royal blue halter dress with a plunging backline. There was a split up each side, revealing her long, muscular legs. It didn't have the bling of her troupe's costume, but she looked stunning all the same. Rory was busy applying her false lashes and then all she needed was a splash of lipstick. She had decided to wear her hair loose for her dance with Ricki, before pinning it up for the Divas performance.

She had to admit, she was glad Ricki had entered them, she was even starting to feel excited. The thrill of being on the stage again—she'd forgotten how that felt. She hadn't thought about entering with Ricki before; he'd shown no interest in competing, so it had come as quite a surprise when he'd announced it this morning. Their category was meant to be choreographed, but she trusted Ricki to lead her through.

"Ten minutes to curtain time!" came a call from off-stage somewhere.

"That's my cue to leave," Rory said, jumping up and down. "Knock 'em dead, hon!" She gave Maddi a quick hug before running out the door to where the audience was sitting. Maddi peered out through the tiny window in the door to the auditorium. It was a full house. Every year, more and more people came to see the show.

"There you are," Ricki said, reaching for her hand. "Wow! You look… amazing." He stood back to admire her.

"Thanks." She blushed. "You look pretty good yourself." She brushed some fluff off his shoulder, smoothing his top.

"Shall we head to the stage? I think we're third up." He offered his arm.

"Sure." She smiled, sliding her arm into his. She took a deep breath to calm the somersaulting butterflies in her stomach.

"What are *you* doing here?" Sacha stepped in front of them. "I didn't think you'd be competing this year, what with you and Dane going your separate ways." She looked back and forth between Ricki and Maddi, her eyes settling on Ricki's chest. "You look good, baby," she crooned, running her hand down his arm. "This look suits you."

"Who said she wasn't competing?" he said, removing her hand.

"I guess I just thought that maybe you'd be tired of her by now." She pouted, leaning into him. "Ready for a real woman, ya know?" She winked.

"Maddi's more woman than you'll ever be." He glared at her. Sacha threw her head back, laughing.

"Oh please. Her? Come and find me when you get bored with little Miss Girl Next Door." She turned on her heel and sashayed away from them.

"God, I hate her," Maddi said through her teeth.

"You and me both," Ricki replied. "Don't let her get to you. We got this." They stepped up to the stage doors.

"Five minutes to curtain! Can I have Sacha and Jessie, Nicole and Rob, and Maddi and Ricki up to the stage first. The next three couples line up down here." He pointed to the space beside the stairs. Everyone rushed around, applying the final touches to their costumes. Some were still rehearsing in the changing rooms, while others sat against the wall, psyching themselves up for their turn on stage. "The list with your order is on the wall over there. Make sure you are ready to go on ahead of time."

"Ladies and Gentlemen! Welcome to the annual National Salsa Championships! I'm Lisa, and I'll be your host tonight. We have three fabulous judges from around the country who have come to watch all our talented performers. Please give them a round of applause!"

Lisa carried on making introductions and listing the order of the show. "Right, so without further ado, it pleases me to announce the first competitors in the advanced section; Sacha Barrett and Jessie Jameson!" The crowd applauded as they took to the stage. Sacha, in her ruby-red dress and fishnets, took up her starting position, giving one final look over her shoulder at Maddi before the intro to their music came on. Maddi recognised it as the same song that they had danced to at Feeney's when Dane had dragged her onto the dancefloor. In fact, the moves they were doing were very much the same. She couldn't believe it. She nudged Ricki, pointing.

"It's the same," she whispered excitedly.

"What do you mean?"

"Their routine. I've seen it before—I practically danced it at Feeney's with them." Ricki watched more closely.

"Oh my God, you're right." He grinned. "We have this in the bag." He rubbed his hands together in glee. He already had a fair idea of what he was going to do when they got out on the stage, including a few surprises he had up his sleeves. While Maddi had been training with the girls, he had been doing some solo practice himself. He had allowed some gaps in the music where he figured they could just freestyle it—they had a great connection after all, but the majority was all planned out. He couldn't wait to see the look on her face when the music started.

"Give it up for Sacha and Jessie!" Lisa called out as she walked across the stage, clapping. They made their way off stage, Sacha brushing up against Ricki as she went past.

"Beat that," she said smugly.

"Please welcome our next competitors! Nicole Marshal and Rob Burdett!"

"Good luck!" Maddi said as they rushed past. They had been in the intermediate section last year. She remembered thinking they were good enough to be in advanced. She cheered them on from the side.

"What are you doing?" Ricki asked.

"Being a good sport." She smiled. "Quite frankly, I don't care where we get in this competition, as long as Sacha doesn't win."

He chuckled. "Sounds good to me." The closing notes of the song rang out. "You ready?"

"As I'll ever be."

"Let's hear it for Nicole and Rob!" The audience clapped and cheered. "And now we have Maddison Lee and her partner Ricki Macavoy!" Lisa bellowed into the mic.

"This is it!" Maddi took a deep breath, plastered a smile on her face and walked out onto the stage. Ricki spun her out and back in to their starting position. The music started. Maddi looked up at Ricki when she realised it was her favourite song. He winked at her.

They began to dance, moving through various combinations and even breaking away to a solo shine. They quite regularly did that when they were dancing at Feeney's, so she was well prepared for it. Ricki pulled out some slick moves she'd never seen before, then pointed at her for her turn. Without hesitating, she threw herself into a deep lunge to the ground, then straightening her legs she rolled her body upwards, followed by an intricate footwork shine. The audience whistled and whooped. Rory hollered, "That's my friend!" which made her smile. They finished off with a lift they had been practicing, where she went up and over his shoulders, sliding down and around his body like a snake. She landed on the floor, her arm extended as she beamed out at the room full of people. She'd done it.

"Make some noise for Maddison and Ricki!" Lisa cried out as she took to the stage once more. Ricki pulled Maddi up and walked her backstage.

"Oh my God! That was amazing!" She threw her arms around his shoulders, and he lifted her in the air.

"I know! What a rush!"

"Nice work, guys!" Piper came running up. "We were watching from the curtains. Did you hear us yelling?"

"I thought that was you." Maddi grinned. "You guys all ready for our section?"

"You betcha! You should probably get organised, though. I don't think there's a lot of time between sections."

"I'll meet you back here after, okay?" Ricki said, squeezing her hand once more before she took off for the changing rooms. "Break a leg!"

The Divas huddled in a circle backstage, waiting for their name to be called.

"Okay, girls, I want you all to know that no matter what happens out there, I'm so proud of you guys. You have made my dream a reality, and I can't thank you enough." She smiled at each of them. "Right, hands in."

She held her hand in the centre of their little circle, and they all placed theirs on top. "Gooooo Divas!"

They strutted out from behind the curtain into their formation. The music began. For a lot of them, this was their first time on stage—not that you could pick it. Just like in rehearsals, they were flawless.

There's something about being under the lights in front of an audience that makes you want to perform to the best of your ability. It gives you such a rush. Hearing the audience cheer and whistle is such a confidence booster.

And then, as quickly as it began, it was over. The Divas held their final positions as the audience continued to clap. Maddi gestured for them to stand, and they strutted back off the stage, hips swaying as they went.

"Alright. Can we have all competitors back on the stage please?" the stage manager yelled. Everyone excitedly moved to the stage door, and up through the curtains, gathering in their groups or couples. Maddi stood between Ricki and the Divas, an arm draped around Piper, and her other hand holding tightly onto Ricki.

The curtains pulled open, and Lisa took centre stage.

"And now, for the moment you have all been waiting for! The results! Judges, have you made your final decisions?" She looked to the judging panel, and they all nodded in agreement. The piece of paper that held their fate was delivered to the stage. "Before we announce the winners, can we have one last round of applause for all our wonderful competitors?" Lisa clapped, turning to smile at everyone behind her.

"And, of course, to our lovely judges for travelling to be with us today, and for being the ones to make the tough decisions." More applause from the audience.

"First up, the teams! We had so many entries for this category, and such variety. I don't envy the judges having to decide this one! In second place, we have…" She paused for effect. "The Latin Divas!"

"Oh my God!" Maddi exclaimed in shock. Her hand flew to her mouth as she looked up at Ricki.

"I knew you could do it!" He smiled at her. "Go get your medal." Piper was almost pulling her arm off as she clung to her, bouncing about excitedly.

"We did it!" she kept screaming.

"Come on up, girls," Lisa said, smiling warmly at Maddi. They shook hands with each of the judges and received their very own medals. They stepped to the side, waiting to hear who had won.

"Congratulations, girls!" Lisa turned back to the audience to announce the winners for the teams' section. Maddi was barely paying attention. She still couldn't believe that her girls had placed. With her routine, no less. It was what she had been working so hard for, and now it was a reality. She was already starting to think about what they would do next when the girls shuffled her back towards the others. They were about to announce the winners of the next section.

She clapped and cheered on her fellow comrades, watching each step forward and take their medals. When it came time to announce the advanced section, Piper grabbed her arm.

"Coming in third place in the advanced section, is… Sacha and Jessie!" Maddi heard Rory boo from off stage and stifled a giggle. She may have placed, but at least she hadn't come in first. It was clear from the look on Sacha's face that she had not been expecting third, and she was *not* happy. She plastered on a fake smile as she and Jessie went up to accept their medals.

Ricki gave Maddi's hand a squeeze, smiling down at her as they waited for the next names to be called out.

"In second place in the advanced section, we have… Nicole and Rob!" Maddi clapped and congratulated them. She made a mental note to catch up with them at the after party. Perhaps they could collaborate for next year.

"And… the winner of the advanced section is… Maddison and Ricki!"

"Yes!" Ricki yelled out as he picked Maddi up and swung her around. She laughed in delight. Two years in a row! And to think, she hadn't even planned on entering. It was all thanks to Ricki, her knight in shining armour.

They went up to accept their medals and a huge bunch of flowers. Rory and Damon were standing right in the front row, cheering them on. Maddi gave a little wave and blew them a kiss.

All the winners gathered around for photos with their medals. Maddi made sure to get some with her girls and promised them all a round of coffee the following morning when everyone had recovered.

Looking around at all her friends, it was easy to forget all the dramas of the past few months. She had been through a lot, but she had come out on top.

Chapter 20

Rory and Damon met them out the front of the auditorium, all ready to party. Rory rushed up to Maddi, sweeping her into a crushing hug.

"You were great!" she cried, the biggest smile across her face. "And you looked so hot in that dress." She nudged her arm.

"Thanks."

"She's right, you're a knock-out. Well done, eh," Damon said, shaking hands with Ricki. "Fucking awesome, mate."

"Thanks, man. It was a bit nerve-wracking, but we made it." He grinned at Maddi.

"Did you see the look on Sacha's face when you won? Priceless!" Rory giggled, imitating her. "I'm surprised she didn't trip over her bottom lip!" Maddi laughed at Rory's re-enactment.

"So now what? You guys wanna go to the party?" Damon asked. Maddi and Ricki exchanged glances.

"Sure, why not?" Maddi said, swinging her arm around Rory's shoulder. "Lead the way."

The after party was bigger than they had expected. It seemed as though every audience member, competitor and their families had turned up to congratulate the winners and join in the celebrations.

Maddi and Ricki had a lot of people coming up to talk to them, asking if they would teach them, or be part of their team for the following year. They caught up with Nicole and Rob and organised to have coffee later in the week to discuss plans for a collaboration.

After a few hours, Maddi had had enough of the festivities, and all she really wanted to do, was go home and hang out with her friends. Once she had sought out Rory and Damon, they made a move for home.

When they got back, they put on some music and Ricki and Maddi attempted to teach them some basic steps. Rory had seen it enough times to pick up the first few moves without any trouble. Damon, on the other hand, had two left feet.

"You know what? How 'bout I just do this?" He bopped up and down. "And you can do your salsa steps around me." He tickled Rory as she swished her hips side to side in front of him.

"That works too." Ricki laughed. He pulled Maddi in, lowering her into a dip. "It's just not as smooth as this though, bro."

"I'll never be as smooth as you, mate." Damon patted his friend on the back. "Who's up for a drink?"

"Ooh I could go for a hot chocolate," Rory piped up.

"Okay, Nana. I was meaning something a little stronger."

"Actually, I could go for a hot chocolate as well," Maddi agreed with a grin. "With marshmallows!" She ran to the cupboard, retrieving the bag she had stowed away.

"Ooh, yes please." Rory snatched them out of her hand, shoving one in her mouth. "I'll put the jug on," she mumbled as she pulled four mugs down from the shelf.

"Alright, hot chocolate it is then," Damon said with a sigh.

"You know you want it," Rory said, shoving yet another marshmallow in her mouth, and then one in his. "Give us a kiss?" She winked at Maddi as she puckered up, gooey marshmallow sticking out. Damon just grinned and kissed her.

"Now that's love," Maddi said, laughing.

"Sure is," Ricki agreed, helping himself to a marshmallow as well. "Give us a kiss?" he said, turning towards Maddi.

"I thought you'd never ask." She grinned, jumping into his arms. She leaned in, their lips almost touching.

"Wait!" cried Rory. "You forgot your marshmallow! Get it right!" She giggled, offering the bag to Maddi.

Without taking her eyes away from Ricki, she reached for the sweet, popping it into her mouth before wrapping her arms around him. They grinned at each other before Ricki slowly lowered his lips to hers.

Thank you for reading my book! *Dancing in Circles* is the first book I wrote, and I had so much fun doing so. If you enjoyed it as much as I enjoyed writing it, then please spare a few minutes to write a review. Reviews help our books to be seen.

Don't forget to grab the final in the series, *Dancing with Destiny.* It's out now!

Thanks!

Stacey Broadbent

Other Books by Stacey Broadbent

Standalone

Never Judge a Book
Deep Heat

A Step in Time Series

Dancing Through the Storm
Dancing in Circles
Dancing with Destiny
A Step in Time: the complete series

Hollywood Novels

Emma

Flesh-Eater Series

Fear the Fever
Fight the Fever

Dark Sins Novellas

Sins of the Flesh
Mine

Ink-Slinging Sisters

Awesome Applesauce

Super Mum Series

Frazzled
Frazzled and Frumpy
Frazzled, Frumpy and Fabulous!
Super Mum: the complete series

Short stories and poetry

Musings, Mournings, and Misadventures

Anthologies

The White Ribbon Collection
Scars to your Beautiful
Witching Hour: Vices and Virtues
Key to my Heart
A Touch of Inspiration
No Place like Home
Serendipity

Acknowledgements

Firstly, I have to thank my amazing friend, Petrina, for having faith in me and pushing me to write this story. I don't know if I could've done it without her. Not only was she my cheerleader, she was also my proofreader, making sure my words were the best they could be.

To all the bloggers who help spread the word of indie authors, you are very much appreciated. We would be lost without you!

Of course, I wouldn't be here without the readers. You are the people who make this all possible. Without you, I couldn't spend my days doing what I love. I appreciate each and every one of you! Thank you for taking the time to read my stories and giving this relatively new author a shot.

Connect with me

http://www.staceybroadbent.weebly.com

https://www.facebook.com/StaceyBroadbentAuthor

Broadbent's Bookish Babes: https://goo.gl/FY9wQN

https://www.amazon.com/author/staceybroadbent

Goodreads: https://goo.gl/YJ6dXa

https://www.instagram.com/authorstaceybroadbent/

https://www.bookbub.com/authors/stacey-broadbent

https://vm.tiktok.com/ZSJBb5bhL/

Sign up for my newsletter:
http://eepurl.com/cULu_f

About the Author

Stacey resides in Ashburton, New Zealand with her husband and three children. She is a qualified proofreader, author, wife, mother, and self-proclaimed culinary goddess. When she's not busy writing or editing books, she enjoys reading and procrastinating on TikTok.

She absolutely loves hearing from readers, so please feel free to reach out via email, Instagram, or join her reader group, Broadbent's Bookish Babes. You can also sign up to her <u>newsletter</u> for up-to-date info on releases.